P9-COO-536

'I'm thinking tomorrow night, you, me, a bottle of good champagne...'

Jason told Angie. 'A roaring fire and a little Rachmaninoff...quiet conversation and easy touching.'

Feminine anticipation fizzed in her veins. But a hint of unease ran beside it. 'Easy touching?'

A knowing smile touched his lips. 'Easy touching means you get to decide when and where and how long it goes on.'

'Do I get a kiss at the end of the night?' Her question was just a little more breathless than she intended, but she couldn't keep the hope and exhilaration from her words.

Jason's nostrils flared wide and his sapphire eyes darkened toward midnight. 'You get whatever you want.'

Available in November 2003 from Silhouette Special Edition

Lt Kent: Lone Wolf

JUDITH LYONS

SILHOUETTE®
SPECIAL EDITION™

DID YOU PURCHASE THIS BOOK WITHOUT A COVER?
If you did, you should be aware it is **stolen property** as it was
reported *unsold and destroyed* by a retailer. Neither the author nor
the publisher has received any payment for this book.

All the characters in this book have no existence outside the imagination
of the author, and have no relation whatsoever to anyone bearing the
same name or names. They are not even distantly inspired by any
individual known or unknown to the author, and all the incidents are
pure invention.

All Rights Reserved including the right of reproduction in whole or in part
in any form. This edition is published by arrangement with Harlequin
Enterprises II B.V. The text of this publication or any part thereof may not
be reproduced or transmitted in any form or by any means, electronic or
mechanical, including photocopying, recording, storage in an
information retrieval system, or otherwise, without the written
permission of the publisher.

This book is sold subject to the condition that it shall not, by way of trade
or otherwise, be lent, resold, hired out or otherwise circulated without the
prior consent of the publisher in any form of binding or cover other than
that in which it is published and without a similar condition including
this condition being imposed on the subsequent purchaser.

Silhouette, Silhouette Special Edition and Colophon are
registered trademarks of Harlequin Books S.A., used under licence.

First published in Great Britain 2003
Silhouette Books, Eton House, 18-24 Paradise Road,
Richmond, Surrey TW9 1SR

© Julie M. Higgs 2001

ISBN 0 373 24398 7

23-1103

Printed and bound in Spain
by Litografia Rosés S.A., Barcelona

JUDITH LYONS

lives in the deep woods in Wisconsin, where anyone who is familiar with the area will tell you one simply cannot survive the bitter winters without a comfortable chair, a cosy fireplace and a stack of good reading. When she decided winters were too cold for training horses and perfect for writing what she loved to read most—romance novels—she put pen to paper and delved into the exciting world of words and phrases and, most important of all, love and romance.

To Ann Voss Peterson and Carol Voss.
Critique partners extraordinaire. Thank you, kind
ladies, for all your tireless help and endless support—
and, most of all, for the laughter that keeps it fun.

Chapter One

All right. So this *wasn't* one of her better ideas.

Angie Rose pulled her foot out of the knee-deep snow drift and plunged it into the next one. Driving snow and ice stung her cheeks and made it nearly impossible to see. Luckily, the narrow, gravel road on which she'd been driving until her rental car had konked out was well marked, so losing her way to Jason Kent's secluded mountain residence wasn't a concern. Freezing to death before she got there? Now *that* was a worry.

Angie shook her hands, trying to get some feeling back into them. Why, she didn't know. Just before they'd gone numb from the cold, the pain had been unbearable.

She shook her head at her stupidity. She should have checked the weather forecast before she had left the hotel this morning, but she'd been too distracted trying to come up with this harebrained scheme. So now she wasn't dressed for a snowstorm, and night was descending rapidly. If she didn't get to Kent's place soon…

She wasn't going to think about that. Lowering her head, she trudged around the next bend, praying that Kent's place would be just around the corner.

And for once in her life she got lucky. Kent's little hideaway came into view the minute she rounded the corner. Except there wasn't anything little about it.

Awe zinged through her. Playing peekaboo through the raging storm was a *gothic mansion*—complete with dark brick, steeply pitched roofs and elaborate, pointy spires reaching toward the sky. A triumphant smile curved her lips, her facial muscles moving stiffly in the cold.

She'd been grasping at straws this morning when she'd decided to do the story on the reclusive Jason Kent instead of the one her magazine, *Excitement Today,* had sent her here to do. But she hadn't known until this moment whether the story would work.

Her smile got a little wider. A gothic mansion on the top of a Montana mountain? Even if Mr. Kent was as dull as bad ad copy she had a story, providing she got to Kent's little hideaway before she froze to death. Ignoring the cold wracking her limbs, she fought her way through the driving winds and drifting snow to the mansion.

Stumbling onto the porch, she stared up at the door knocker mounted on the solid oak door. The brass fixture was shaped like a gargoyle, and the little beastie was glaring down at her with sinister malevolence burning in his eyes.

Hopefully, the charming little monster didn't reflect Kent's attitude toward visitors, because she was here— and in this storm she wasn't leaving. Her fingers too numb to curl around the knocker, she pushed the buzzer next to the door instead. Chimes as resonant as those found in old churches rang around her, both inside and outside the mansion. Excitement flowed through her.

A recluse. A mansion straight out of *The Hunchback of Notre Dame*. And Bela Lugosi music floating through the walls. Story city. She waited anxiously for someone to answer the door.

But no one came.

She pushed the bell again. "Come on, Lurch. Answer the door, I'm freezing out here."

"WHO IS IT?" An angry voice boomed around her.

Angie almost jumped out of her skin. Quickly scanning the walls, she found the speakers on the wall to her right. Okay, so Jason Kent *didn't* greet visitors with open arms. He growled at them from behind closed doors, no doubt hoping the mansion's appearance, the eerie music and his werewolf impression would scare them away. But leaving wasn't an option.

Struggling with her numb, stiff fingers, she pushed the button next to the intercom. "Mr. Kent? It's Angie Rose. I was due at Kent House this evening. But I seem to have taken the wrong road." A lie.

She'd been sent here to do an article on Kent House, a group home Jason Kent had built for hard-to-adopt children, but she'd known right from the beginning she wasn't going to do that story. There was no way she could face a room full of orphans and walk away with her heart intact. So this morning she'd come up with the Jason Kent angle. Surely her editor would be just as happy with a story on the recluse who'd built the orphanage.

If he ever let her in. She waited for his response, the cold seeping further into her bones.

Silence.

Unable to suppress a shiver, she pushed the intercom

button again. "*Excitement Today* sent me, Mr. Kent. I'm writing an in-depth article on Kent House."

The intercom crackled to life. "I KNOW WHO YOU ARE, MS. ROSE. GO BACK DOWN THE MOUNTAIN AND STAY ON THE PAVED ROAD."

Angie jumped again. The growl was just as loud, just as unwelcoming this time around. She closed her eyes against the sudden panic that Jason Kent might *not* let her in.

She swallowed hard and pressed the button again. "I can't go back, Mr. Kent. My car is broken down. And— have you looked out your window lately? There's this huge storm out here."

Silence.

Oh dear. She could be in serious trouble. She tried again. "Mr. Kent, when I left my hotel this morning I didn't know this storm was coming. And I didn't know my car would break down and leave me stranded. All I have on is a light coat and jeans and *tennis* shoes."

Silence.

She dropped her head against the brick wall. *All right.* This was the *worst* idea she'd ever had. But she was stuck with it. And dang it, so was Mr. Kent.

She punched the button again. "Mr. Kent, did I mention that my car gave up the ghost about two miles down the road? I've been wading through this snow for about forty-five minutes now. My tennies are wet. My jeans are wet. And I don't have on any gloves. Hypothermia is only about ten seconds away. Could you *please* open the door?" She wasn't surprised to hear either the desperation in her voice or the chattering of her teeth.

The intercom crackled again. "HOLD ON."

Relief poured through her. He was coming. He wasn't happy about it. Anger had vibrated in the growled command. But he was coming. She waited, wondering what the cranky Mr. Kent would look like.

Old, she decided. The intercom system had made Mr. Kent's words boom, but the voice itself had not been robust. It had been scratchy and rough. Old. And that crankiness? Only old men were that crotchety. Eccentric old men.

Finally, *finally* the door swung open.

The first thing Angie noticed was the cane. The staff was made of deep, rich mahogany and it was topped by a gold handle. A gold handle shaped like an eagle, its wings spread wide, its beak open in an angry cry. The second thing Angie noticed was the hand wrapped around the eagle.

It wasn't old.

The skin was supple. The fingers long and strong. She lifted her gaze from that hand and moved up a well muscled arm to Jason Kent's face.

Definitely not old.

Mid-thirties. Tops. A strong take-no-prisoners jaw. Raven-black hair. High, ruggedly carved cheekbones. And eyes the color of sapphires. It was a profile that had her heart pumping.

And the body attached to that face? *Oh, baby.* Dressed in sharply creased chinos and a neatly tucked-in white Polo shirt, Jason Kent stood an easy six foot one with broad shoulders, narrow hips and a military bearing that screamed finely honed strength and pure male power.

Forget the mansion, the story was standing right in front of her.

"I thought you were ten seconds from hypothermia, Ms. Rose. Do you plan on standing out there until you succumb?"

Angie jerked her gaze back to the man's face. He

frowned. And it looked as if those roughly growled words were the only invitation she was going to get.

Before he could slam the door in her face she stepped by him into the foyer. The mansion's warmth grazed her cheeks, but she barely noticed it. She'd walked straight into the middle ages.

Or an old horror movie.

The walls; the floor; the high, arched ceiling; even the two massive staircases, curving up to a second story from opposite sides of the enormous hall, were made of chiseled gray stone.

Beautifully carved stone ribs covered every seam in the room's construction, creating a delicate, lacy web that would have given the room an air of majestic beauty if there had been any attempt to soften the effect of the cold gray stone. But with the exception of a brass coatrack sitting by the door, the cavernous hall was empty.

The door whooshed shut behind her, sending a blast of frigid air into the hall and blocking out the natural light that had provided much of the room's illumination. She turned back to Jason Kent, a nervous tremor skidding up her spine.

And one look at him turned that tremor into a silent scream. Before she could stop herself she gasped in horror and took a step back. A long, arcing scar, starting at his lip, slicing over his cheek bone and slashing through the outer corner of his eye marred the side of his face that she hadn't been able to see when he'd opened the door.

A cold, self-deprecating laugh slipped from his lips. "What's wrong, Ms. Rose? Not as pretty a picture as you thought?"

Appalled at her unguarded reaction she clenched her fists and resisted the urge to take another step back.

A mocking smile twisted his lips. "Are you sure you want to stay? You could rush back into the storm."

Angie tried to calm the pounding of her heart. It was only a scar. It might look monstrous, but it didn't *make* him a monster. And if he was scowling at her right now, it was her own fault. She'd shown up on his doorstep uninvited and then gasped at his appearance as if he were the devil himself.

If everyone reacted to his scars the way she had, no wonder the man didn't want visitors. Mustering her courage she met his gaze squarely. "I'm sorry, Mr. Kent. I shouldn't have reacted that way."

He stared at her silently, his dark blue gaze unwavering.

She shifted uncomfortably. "I know you didn't ask me up here, and you have every reason to want me gone. But with that storm out there I am truly stuck."

His eyes narrowed suspiciously. "How *did* you get stuck here, Ms. Rose? My road is well hidden. Most people drive by without even seeing it."

She imagined they did. The road that headed up the side of the mountain to Kent House had been a real road. Two lanes. Pavement. But the road that led up Jason Kent's side of the mountain had been no more than a glorified jeep path discreetly tucked between towering pines.

But she'd been looking for it—a fact she wasn't about to share. She was pretty sure if she told him she'd come up here for a story, she'd find herself hiking back down the mountain. Storm or no storm.

But he obviously wasn't going to believe she'd taken the road by mistake. She scrambled for a legitimate reason to have wandered off the main road. "You're right. I bet most people drive right by, but I—I like exploring." *Yeah.* "And narrow, hidden roads snaking into the great un-

known are just more than I can resist." Let him argue
with that.

He looked at her hard, gauging the truth of her words.
Finally he must have decided there was at least a possibility she was telling the truth because he bent his head
in a single, succinct nod. "I'd curb that inclination while
you're in Montana if I were you. Wandering onto property
uninvited can get you shot here." His tone was as dry as
prairie grass in September.

With a soft sigh of relief, she nodded her head vigorously. "I will. I promise."

He acknowledged her assurance with another quick nod
and pointed to a set of big, open double doors to her left.
"There's a fire through there. Go stand in front of it while
I fix you something hot to drink. If the blue tinge to your
lips means anything, you were right about the hypothermia. You're teetering on the edge." With that curt command he turned away from her and headed across the
large foyer, his uneven gait and the tap of his cane echoing from one gray stone wall to the next.

A shiver skittered up her spine. She'd come up here
looking for a story. And she'd found one. But the whole
scenario was a little unnerving. The weather. The mansion. Jason Kent.

Jason Kent.

A knot of uncertainty hardened in her stomach. With his
military bearing and acrimonious attitude the man was as
intimidating as a four-star general with a loaded weapon
and no war to fight. Getting personal information out of
him for her story might be tougher than she'd thought.

Jason made his way down the dark corridor to the
kitchen, frustration clawing at his gut. He didn't want her
here. This was *his* refuge.

He'd originally bought the mansion so he'd have a quiet place to unwind after missions—a place where he didn't have to think about the delicate balance of power between countries and corporations and greedy men who wanted to rule the world and were willing to sacrifice innocent people to do it. But after his last mission had gone so wrong the mansion had become a different kind of refuge.

A place to hide.

A place where he didn't have to face the fear and scorn and pity of those who saw only the scar and the limp. Where he didn't have to face the look he'd seen on Ms. Rose's face only moments before. One he'd probably see a thousand times while the curious explorer was under his roof.

Unfortunately, he couldn't just hand the woman her tea and shuffle her back out into the cold. The weathermen were already calling this the worst storm in a hundred years. The raging winds and falling snow were supposed to go on for the next three days. And cleanup to open the roads would take just as long.

He pulled a mug from the cupboard, filled it with water and shoved it into the microwave. A week. It would be a damned week before the snowplow made it up his road.

He gave a bitter laugh as he punched the timer button. Snowbound with a beautiful woman for a week. Every man's fantasy.

Jason's hands tightened into fists. Even standing on his porch looking like a snow-encrusted, drowned rat her beauty had been apparent. Her tall, lithe body had just enough curve to spike a man's imagination. Make him wonder just how soft she would be with all the trappings peeled away. And her face was even more striking than her body. Wide, high cheekbones. Almond shaped eyes tilted up at the corners. And bee-stung lips that made a man sweat just thinking about what they'd feel like...

Jason closed his eyes against the tantalizing picture. This wasn't a fantasy come true. Ms. Rose's lips wouldn't get anywhere near him. Hers or any other woman's. Along with ending his career, his "little mishap" had ensured that no woman would ever look his way again. A fact he'd thought he'd learned to live with, until the lovely Ms. Rose had shown up on his doorstep. Her soft curves and kiss-me lips had reminded him in a hurry of exactly what he'd been missing.

And her look of horror when she'd seen the scarred side of his face had reminded him just as quickly, and far more brutally, exactly how women saw him now.

The microwave's bell pinged in the kitchen's silence. Jason jerked himself out of his dark musings. He couldn't change the past. And he couldn't save the future. But thanks to this old relic of a mansion he could put a fair amount of distance between himself and Ms. Rose.

He pulled the hot water from the microwave and dropped a tea bag into the cup. He'd pour the tea down her, let her warm up by the fire and then he'd shuffle her off to the other side of this giant pile of rocks. If he didn't see her, he wouldn't have to think about her. About her, or about just how much he'd lost at that little South American bridge three years ago.

Chapter Two

Jason returned to the study, tea in hand. The little adventurer had tossed her purse on the couch and now she stood in front of the giant fireplace, hands stretched out to the flames. But she was still wearing her coat. And she was still shivering.

"You're not going anywhere, Ms. Rose. Take your coat off so the heat can get to you."

She turned at the sound of his voice, frustration and misery pulling the lines of her face tight. "I can't take it off. I can't get hold of the zipper." She raised her hands and tried to move her fingers. An angry red from the cold, they resisted her every attempt.

He set the tea on a side table and moved to her as quickly as he could. "Let me get it."

She raised her chin, her teeth chattering like little jackhammers, the tiny movement stirring the air around her, filling it with her scent.

His nostrils flared wide and before he could stop himself he drew the scent in like a dying man taking that last breath of sweet air. The storm, sweet jasmine and the subtle, intoxicating scent of woman flooded his senses.

His fingers flexed on the zipper. It had been three years since he'd been near a woman. Three long years. A lifetime. But only the bare tip of the iceberg if he considered the years that stretched before him. Years that offered nothing more than bleak solitude and his own deranged ramblings. No days filled with a wife's easy companionship nor nights filled with a woman's passionate touch nor hallways filled with children's laughter. Just endless silence in this cold pile of stones.

He ruthlessly pushed the desolate thoughts aside. He needed Ms. Rose out of here. Out of his study and tucked away in the farthest corner of this pitiful mausoleum where her mere presence wouldn't remind him of the dreams that had been slashed and shattered along with his face and knee. He slipped the zipper down and pulled the soaking wet coat from her in one quick motion. And froze in his tracks.

Ms. Rose's clothes were as soaked as the jacket hanging from his suddenly numb fingers. The wet material clung to her like a second skin, defining her every curve, her every hollow, her every seductive shape.

Desire crashed through him, full-blown and needy. He gritted his teeth against the unwelcome response and wondered how quickly he could get her warmed up and tucked out of his sight. He glanced at her again. Not any time soon in those clothes. They were actually dripping on the floor.

He tried to keep the impatience from his voice as he addressed the wayward traveler. ''You're not going to get any warmer as long as you're wearing those wet clothes,

Ms. Rose. They're wicking away your body heat quicker than you're making it. You're going to have to strip down and put something dry on.''

She wrapped her arms around herself, trying to hoard what warmth she had left. ''I don't have anything dry. My car is two miles down the road, remember?''

Damn. He hadn't remembered. His mind had been otherwise occupied since he'd opened the door and found a beautiful woman standing on his porch. He cast his gaze desperately around the study as if by sheer force of will he could make a woman's wardrobe appear. Not even a blanket came into view. Finally the door that led to the gym caught his eye.

He looked back to Ms. Rose, pointing to the door behind his desk. ''There's a gym through there with a heavy terry cloth robe hanging near the shower. That'll keep you warm until we get your clothes dry.''

Her shoulders slumped in relief and a hesitant smile crossed her lips. ''Thanks.'' She hurried across the study as quickly as her cold, stiff body would allow.

It took a small struggle and both her hands to open the gym's door, but she managed. He breathed a sigh of relief as the door shut behind her. The next time he saw her she'd be wrapped in a ratty old robe a good four sizes too big. There wouldn't be a curve left.

Thank God.

He looked around the room, feeling like a caged animal. Normally he enjoyed being in his study. In fact, this was his favorite room in the house. With its tuck-and-rolled leather sofa, wing chair, rich mahogany coffee table and the giant, Montana-size desk he'd picked out himself, this room was more him than any other. But right now he'd give all his wealth to be somewhere else. Anywhere else.

He shifted his attention to the fire, watching the crackling flames and wondering how long he'd have to torture himself by being in Ms. Rose's presence tonight. But then inspiration struck. There were several places throughout this old mansion where the craftsmanship was excellent. The giant fireplace in front of him was one of them. Its elaborately carved stone mantel was an impressive work of art, but he'd always thought the enormous size of the fire pit overkill.

Until now. Now it would be his salvation. He moved to the stack of wood piled directly next to the fireplace, leaned his cane against the carved stone mantel and started pitching logs into the flames like a man possessed. He'd build the small fire he'd laid earlier into a blazing inferno that would warm Ms. Rose up in five seconds flat.

The fire, already burning hot, leapt to life at the new fuel, its blue and orange flames growing higher and higher. By the time the gym door opened, the blaze was scorching hot even ten feet from the flames.

He glanced toward the gym. Ms. Rose stood in the open doorway wrapped in the heavy folds of his robe, the long belt pulled snug at her waist. While the robe thankfully hid most of her curves, it unfortunately left some quite exposed.

The collar gaped wide, displaying the top swell of her breasts. Even from across the room the alluring curves looked soft and inviting and so damned touchable. He snapped his gaze away from the tempting sight and settled it on her face.

Her teeth were still chattering to beat hell.

Damn. The woman was freezing to death in his study while he drooled over her like a boy who'd just discovered breasts. Had his accident stripped him of all decency? "You're not going to get warm over there, Ms. Rose.

Come over by the fire.'' The anger he felt at himself filled his voice.

And Ms. Rose obviously thought the anger was for her. She stood in the doorway nibbling nervously on those full, sumptuous lips, staring at his scarred face and trying to decide if he was friend or foe. Or maybe she was nervous about something else.

Like discovery. In all the years he'd lived here no one had ever accidentally wandered up his road before. Maybe she hadn't, either. Maybe she'd wanted more than a story on Kent House. Maybe she'd come to get a story on him. He'd had more than one reporter ask him for an interview in the past—requests he'd always turned down. But maybe the lovely Ms. Rose was the type of reporter willing to go to any lengths—even subterfuge—to get her story.

He gave a mental snort. What an arrogant ass. If she'd wandered up his road on a bright, summer day, suspecting that she might be after a story would be reasonable. But in the middle of a killer snowstorm? He wasn't that important.

No, her nervousness no doubt came from his frightening visage. He gave a frustrated sigh. ''Despite my threatening appearance I don't eat small children, Ms. Rose. Or their older counterparts. Come get warm.''

Embarrassment bloomed on her cheeks. And then impatience flashed in her hazel eyes. At him? At herself? He didn't know, but the next thing he knew she tipped her chin up and stepped out from behind his desk, her tread light and silent on the thick oriental carpets, her breasts jiggling softly beneath the worn cotton of his robe.

A silent groan echoed through his head. He didn't need to think about jiggling breasts. Or about her bare skin warming the inside of his robe. He jerked his gaze to the floor and stared at the intricate design woven into the rug. Not a single tantalizing image there. He drew in a deep, calming breath.

And then ten of the most audacious toes he'd ever seen stepped into his view. Pretty little toes with perfectly manicured toenails sporting the brightest red nail polish he'd ever seen. Let's-dance-until-dawn red. And those ten audacious little toes were attached to two of the daintiest, most feminine feet he'd ever seen.

Another groan echoed through his head. Feminine, dainty *feet?* What the hell was wrong with him? Feet didn't turn anybody on. And if they were turning him on now, he was in deeper trouble than he'd thought.

He grabbed his cane and moved away from the fire, giving her a wide berth. Being anywhere near her was obviously more than he could handle. He moved to the couch and dropped into its leathery folds.

She stood in front of the fireplace, her hands spread out to the flames, shifting nervously from one pretty little foot to the other. No surprise there. She was no doubt wondering if his scars just made him hideously ugly or were a reflection of his soul.

He could reassure her. Tell her he meant her no harm, but he knew from experience that the words wouldn't have much effect. And pride kept them from crossing his lips at any rate.

He was the same man who had opened the door to her. She hadn't been afraid then, when she couldn't see the scarred side of his face. In fact, the feminine interest sparkling in those lovely eyes had been as clear as the snow falling from the sky. Her alarm hadn't appeared until she'd seen the scar.

Awkward silence stretched out as he watched her warming herself. She looked small and vulnerable standing next to the massive mantle, his ratty robe brushing the tops of those pretty little feet.

Finally she peeked over her shoulder and found him watching her. A pink stain colored her cheeks and she turned to him, an over-bright smile on her face. She seemed to grapple for something to say for a few seconds, and then she pointed back to the carving in the center of the mantle. "This fellow reminds me of the one on your door. Do you have gargoyles lurking in every corner?"

He shrugged, thinking of all the gargoyles in the mansion. "There's at least one in every room and a whole platoon of them guarding the eaves." He used to look upon the odd figures with amusement, but now his feelings alternated between a strange kind of kinship and jealousy.

Their frightening faces and oftentimes weak bodies reminded him of himself. But whereas the small monsters had guarded and protected this mansion and its human inhabitants for the last eight hundred years and would continue to do so for the next eight hundred, his days of soldiering were over.

Ms. Rose seemed to relax a little at his easy answer. "Are they all so fierce? This one looks as if he's trying to scare everyone away." Her fingers were working better now and she grasped the lapels of his robe, pulling them closed over her chest, hoarding the warmth she'd gained from the fire.

Which was fine with him. Now he wouldn't even be tempted to peek. "In the twelfth century people believed gargoyles warded off evil spirits. I imagine the man who built this place wanted to make sure his sentinels were mean enough to drive off even the most vicious spirits."

A single, graceful brow winged toward her hairline. "The *twelfth* century?"

He nodded, letting the implication sink in.

"*This* mansion was built in the twelfth century?"

"Yes."

She narrowed her eyes on him, her reporter's skepticism coming to the fore. "Not in America it wasn't."

He had to smile. "No, not in America. It was built around 1180 in a small hamlet in Germany."

Those lovely almond-shaped eyes went wide, their hazel depths glistening with awe as they once again took in the room, this time from a whole new perspective. She turned to him, avid curiosity brightening her face, her uneasiness with him all but forgotten in her excitement. "How did it get *here?*"

He understood her enthusiasm. He too had been fascinated with the mansion once. But it had lost its magic three years ago when he'd realized he'd never share its uniqueness with a wife and family. The beauties of the place faded from his notice then. Now all he saw was the gray stone. The cold, gray stone.

"A man by the name of Drescher had it moved here at the turn of the century—every stone, every pane of colorful glass, every gargoyle."

"Wow." She turned back to the gargoyle and ran a finger reverently over the carved stone. "It's hard to imagine someone carving this face eight hundred years ago. Someone who believed the image would actually protect the room."

She whirled back toward him and strode over to the couch, all her trepidation gone as she got caught up in the story. She dropped down into the opposite corner of the couch, pulled her knees up to her chest and wrapped the robe around her legs. "Tell me more."

Oh no. He took one look at those pretty little candy-apple-red toenails peeking out from his robe, and he knew he was on dangerous ground. This little scene was way too cozy.

It was one thing for her to land on his doorstep and remind him how much he missed the feel of a woman's soft skin, the sweet scent of her filling his senses. But it was quite another for her to sit down on his couch and remind him of just how lonely the last thousand nights of his life had been. Just how lonely the next thousand would be. *That* torture he could live without.

Using the cane and his one good leg, he pushed himself up from the couch. "As much as I'd love to sit around and chat with you, Ms. Rose, I have pressing matters that need attending. I'll show you to your room. Now that you're warm, you can rest there until dinner. I'm sure walking up the mountain through the storm has worn you out."

She tensed at his curt words, her expression once again wary as, no doubt, she tried once more to decide if he was man or monster.

He didn't want to know her answer. He pivoted on his good leg and headed out of the study. "I'd follow if I were you, Ms. Rose. It's an easy house to get lost in."

He'd barely taken four steps when he heard her push herself up from the couch and fall in step behind him. "What about my clothes?"

"Leave them. I'll throw them in the dryer while you're resting. You can put them on before dinner."

Her bare feet padded behind him as he led her into the deeply shadowed foyer and toward the stone staircases climbing up the adjacent wall. Each staircase led to its own separate hall, its own separate set of rooms.

He should take Ms. Rose up the right staircase. Along with his armory all of the guest rooms occupied that hall. Most important, his set of rooms *didn't* occupy that hall.

But when he should have turned to take her up the right set of stairs, his legs kept going straight. Straight to the left-hand staircase, up the stairs and down the hall to the room directly opposite his own bedroom. Where he stood, defeated.

Defeated by his own foolish need to know he wasn't the only human rattling around in this cold pile of stones. And his need to smell sweet jasmine mixed with the heady scent of woman.

He mentally shook his head. He was the biggest fool to walk God's green earth. Having her this close would only torture him. But she was here now and unless he wanted to look like a complete madman, turning around and taking her to the other hall wasn't an option.

Of course, once she saw the room he was about to settle her into she would wonder about his sanity anyway. Certainly, she would wonder about his masculinity. But for a few days of knowing he wasn't the only one wandering around this mountain of rubble, he could live with that.

He turned the knob and pushed the door open. "The bathroom is the third door down on the right, Ms. Rose. I believe you'll find everything else you need in the room. Dinner's at six."

Angie watched Jason Kent make his way back to the stairs, the tap of his cane echoing through the hall. She wasn't sure what to think about the man. He was clearly not happy about having an uninvited guest show up on his doorstep—and he'd shown few qualms about expressing that displeasure.

But he'd extended her every courtesy, right down to sharing his clothes. He'd even made her a cup of tea. Which they'd both forgotten about and left on the end table untouched. But he'd made it and brought it to her just the same.

Reluctantly, she had to admit that his scarred face was a big part of the uneasiness she felt around him. True, his abrupt manner reinforced that uneasiness. But would his curtness have bothered her so much without his scar?

She doubted it. Which meant that she had to look beyond it. Particularly if she wanted to get the real Jason Kent on the page for her readers. So tonight at dinner, she'd look beyond the scar to the man beneath.

A sudden shiver skated through her. She glanced down at her bare feet on the stone floors. No wonder she was cold. She hurried into the bedroom, anxious to get her bare feet on the thick oriental rugs strewn across the floor. Closing the door behind her she glanced around the room. Awe stopped her dead.

Beautifully crafted white-and-gold French provincial furniture filled the room. Beveled mirrors hung from several of the stone walls, catching the light and reflecting it back into the room in glittering pieces. A huge, floor-to-ceiling, mullioned window on her left copied the act with its own multitude of tiny panes, the combined effect making it seem as if a thousand diamonds had been tossed into the air. And the most amazing thing of all?

Everything was upholstered or draped or decorated in pink. *Pink.*

She shook her head in wonder. *What* was a room like this doing in Jason Kent's mansion? The question boggled her mind. The man was too…too…male to have a room of such feminine fancy in his house. Even if the room had been here when he bought the place she couldn't imagine him leaving it intact.

If her two older brothers had bought a house when they'd been living the bachelor's life, and it had a room like this, there would have been a giant pile of gold and white and pink on the curb by morning.

Another cold chill shook her. Despite its luxury, the room was cold. There was a fireplace on the far wall, but no fire burned there. And the ever-present gray stones filled every corner of the room with their cold, damp presence.

She stared at the giant canopied bed holding center court in the enormous room. The pink down comforter looked snuggly. And warm. Without a second thought, she raced to the bed, scrambled up and pulled the thick comforter over her. Her heat caught in the folds and within seconds turned the pink froth of cotton into a warm cocoon. That fun little hike up Kent's mountain had definitely taxed her. Kent was right, a short rest before dinner would do her a world of good.

She took one last look around the amazing room. Okay, at dinner she'd look beyond his scar. She'd find the real person beneath. And then she'd ask about this room. Because there was a story here. One she couldn't wait to hear.

Chapter Three

All right, so her little ordeal in the storm had worn her out more than she'd thought and she'd slept through dinner. A mistake she'd be careful *not* to make in the future. Because creeping through this old mansion in the middle of the night was definitely not her idea of fun.

She scanned the dark, unfamiliar hallway, her heart pounding anxiously against her ribs. Her imagination had always been…active, as her family said. And this old mansion definitely spurred it on. Even last evening, with some natural light coming through the windows and several lights burning, the mansion had been deeply shadowed. But in the middle of the night it was a veritable pit of darkness and menacing innuendo.

She'd slipped down this hallway from the foyer because it was the biggest, and she figured the kitchen was important enough to warrant a major spot in the mansion. She hoped she was right; her heart wasn't going to take much more of this. Every time she rounded a corner or walked by an open door she expected to run into an angry ghost with blood still dripping from his wounds or his head floating an unnatural distance from his shoulders.

She stopped in front of the first door in the hall, praying it was the kitchen and not the favorite haunting place of some raging phantom. She took a deep, fortifying breath and shoved the door open.

The shadowy shape of a counter loomed about ten feet in front of her. *Yes.* She slipped in, shut the door behind her, fumbled for the wall switch and flicked it on. Light flooded the room.

She leaned back against the door with a relieved sigh. She'd made it, safe and sound, without encountering a single spectral entity. She chuckled softly. There was plenty of light in here to keep the ghosts away. She stared at the state-of-the-art kitchen that stretched before her, marveling at the combination of ancient architecture and modern technology.

Whoever had designed this room had intertwined the two ages with sheer artistry. Track lighting flooded the kitchen with light without obscuring the arches overhead. The soft curves of the white, modern-day counters were the perfect counterpoint to the sharp angles of the ancient architecture. And off to the side a small table with two chairs sat cozily in front of a leaded glass window.

Her stomach growled into the room's silence, nudging her into action. An omelette sounded good. Surely Jason Kent wouldn't mind if she whipped up an omelette. She pushed away from the door and strode into the kitchen. She needed a big mixing bowl and a wire whisk. And eggs, of course.

She located the bowl quickly enough; there was one sitting out on the counter. She was opening and closing drawers, searching for the whisk, when the kitchen door creaked behind her. Despite her decision that no ghosts would visit this room, she spun around at the sound, expecting anything from a bloody apparition to the headless horseman to come screaming in.

But what she found was Jason Kent standing in the open door.

She slapped her hand over her racing heart. "You scared me to death." And the scowl on his face wasn't doing much to slow the pounding of her heart.

A single brow winged toward his hair line. "My apologies. Should I hang bells around my neck so you'll have plenty of time to scurry away before I show up?"

Ouch. What was that about? She suddenly felt like a guest who'd overstepped her bounds. She awkwardly held up the bowl. "I'm sorry. I was hungry, and I didn't think you'd mind if I fixed myself an omelette."

The corners of his mouth tightened. "You needn't sneak around in the middle of the night to feed yourself, Ms. Rose. Or hide in your room to avoid my company. I may look like a monster, but I assure you, I'm not."

Now she understood that last stinging remark about the bells. And his foul mood. She hurried to reassure him. "I'm sorry I missed dinner. Hiking up your hill yesterday just wore me out. I crawled into that gorgeous bed…and was out like a light. Then when I woke up, I was starving. I didn't think you'd mind if I wandered down and raided the fridge."

He stood silently, no doubt trying to decide if she was telling the truth.

Maybe a peace offering would help. She nodded at the bowl. "Should I make enough for two?"

"You're a guest here, Ms. Rose. If you're hungry I'll be happy to fix you an omelette."

Guest? Yeah, right. She wrinkled her nose at him. "Actually, I think I'm more an intruder. Why don't you let me fix them? I'm quite accomplished at it, really."

"Do you think I'm incapable of making an omelette, Ms. Rose, just because I need a cane to get from point A to point B?" Irritation sounded in his rough voice as he scowled at her from across the room, the scars turning the frown into something dark and fierce.

Her hands tightened around the metal bowl. And then she caught it. The flash of frustrated anger in those sapphire blue eyes. God, why hadn't she noticed it earlier? He wasn't angry at her. He was angry at himself. Himself and life's nasty little twists of fate.

She should have recognized his crossness as a defense mechanism last night. Lord knew, after her car accident five years ago she'd practiced the art of self-defense with religious zeal herself. She mentally shook her head. How many times had she lashed out at her family? Lashed out at every imagined slight? Every careless word her family had uttered? Hundreds.

Because she hadn't seen beyond her loss at the time. And she'd been positive no one else could, either. She'd thought everyone who looked at her saw exactly what she did when she looked in the mirror. Someone who was less than she had been. Someone who would never be whole again. And she'd *hated* it.

She studied the scar arcing across Kent's face. It wasn't brand new. The pink tinge of a freshly healing wound was gone, but she'd bet it wasn't very old, either. The pain in his eyes was still too fresh. Too raw.

It had taken her a couple of years to move beyond those crippling emotions. She wished a much quicker recovery for Jason Kent. And in the meantime, she'd be careful not to do anything he could misconstrue as an affront to either his disfigurement or his capabilities. But she wouldn't coddle him, either. Her family had babied her to death, and it had only made her feel twice as helpless, a hundred times more afflicted. And it had allowed her to wallow in her self-pity way too long.

She met Mr. Kent's dark blue gaze. "The cane has nothing to do with it, Mr. Kent. I was the one who missed dinner and therefore woke up hungry in the middle of the night. It didn't even occur to me to hunt you down and drag you out of bed to feed me. But now that you're here…" She slid the bowl toward him with a cocky grin. "By all means, have at it."

He stared at her, wondering, probably, whether she was being sincere or patronizing.

She kept her gaze steady and true.

Finally, he seemed to choose in her favor, some of the angry tension flowing out of him. He moved into the kitchen, his cane tapping on the stone floor.

She moved away from the counter to give him room, but she hadn't gone three steps when the possible ramifications of her actions occurred to her. Her stomach clenched in hunger and her pace faltered. She looked back to him. "You do know how to make an omelette, don't you?"

He raised a sardonic brow. "Afraid it will be inedible?"

"Well, I'm not trying to be sexist here. But most of the men I know fumble over a peanut-butter-and-jelly sandwich."

"I can't guarantee my peanut-butter-and-jelly sandwiches; I haven't made one in years. But I make omelettes all the time. You'll find it edible and then some."

Relief poured through her and she gave him a beaming smile. "All righty then. You won't mind if I fix a pot of coffee though, will you?'' She pointed to the coffeemaker. ''If a man's going to cook for me, I want to be able sit back, sip a good cup of coffee and really enjoy the experience.''

To her greater relief and surprise, a hint of a smile pulled at his lips. ''By all means, have at it. Coffee's in the fridge.''

She moved to the refrigerator and opened the door. She blinked once. Twice. But the contents didn't change. She stared at the multiple shelves of beverages. And only beverages. Milk, soda, a couple of different brands of imported beer, a gazillion different kinds of fruit juices and a virtual plethora of gourmet coffees.

Pretty darned impressive. But where was his food? She leaned around the door to ask, but he'd disappeared. She spied an open metal door, the type of door that usually led to a giant meat locker or a commercial refrigerator. She strode across the kitchen and peered through the open door.

Yep, a walk-in fridge. And Jason Kent was standing in the back of it surrounded by shelves overflowing with every kind of food one could imagine. Fruits, vegetables, eggs, butter, a whole shelf of smoked meats and another shelf filled with exotic cheeses still sealed tight in their wax skins. So this is how the rich and eccentric lived.

She stepped inside the cold, stainless-steel chamber. ''Well, I guess we won't have to worry about starving to death. Even if this storm lasts until spring.''

He glanced over his shoulder at her, his expression wry. ''And aren't you glad?''

She chuckled softly. ''You have no idea. I get so cranky when I'm hungry.''

He raised a brow. ''Then *I'm* glad I'm fully stocked. What do you want in your omelette?''

She eyed the shelf filled with cheese. "Got any gruyere over there?"

He reached over, snatched up a wedge of cheese and dropped it into the metal bowl he'd obviously grabbed from where she'd left it on the counter. "What else?"

She looked at the veggies next to her. It didn't take her long to find what she was looking for. She picked up the small cardboard box of mushrooms and waggled it in front of him.

He took the box and put it in the bowl with the cheese. "Onions?"

She wrinkled her nose.

He raised a brow. "I take it that's a no."

"Well, if you want them," she conceded with a dramatic sigh.

He shook his head. "I can live without them." He turned back to the full shelves and started putting eggs in the bowl.

Rather ingenious, she thought. He could carry quite a few supplies in the bowl and still manage his cane. No wonder the bowl had been sitting out.

He glanced over his shoulder at her. "Weren't you making coffee?"

She smiled again. "Yes, I was." She spun on her heel and went back to her task.

By the time he had the mushrooms sautéing in a pan of butter and dry Vermouth she was sitting at the little table in front of the window with a cup of coffee in her hands. She took a sip of the dark brew and quietly watched him.

He was grating the cheese, the muscles beneath his shirt flexing with a strength and subtlety that triggered a purely feminine response in her. And his hands... She'd always been a sucker for a man's hands. Kent's long, strong fingers moved with a speed and dexterity that made the blood sing through her veins. How would they feel, she wondered, stroking over…

She jerked herself from those tantalizing thoughts. She'd quit thinking about the pleasure a man's hands could create when she'd been forced to choose a career over a personal relationship and family. And now was not the time for dwelling on what could never be, particularly since her future career might well hinge on writing this man's story. And speaking of that story…

Kent had closed her out last night when she'd started digging for details on the mansion. Maybe she'd have better luck now. She lowered her cup to the table, wrapped her hands around its warm surface and made her voice sound as casual as she could. "Tell me how you found this house. Were you looking for something like this? Or did you just stumble onto it?"

He looked up from what he was doing, humor sparkling in his eyes, the hint of a smile pulling at his lips. "An authentic gothic mansion in the high Rockies? Yeah, I was looking for that."

She chuckled softly. All right, the dumbest question ever asked. But it had made the man smile, and she liked that. She imagined he'd done little smiling since his accident. "Let me rephrase. How *did* you end up here, on this mountain, in this mansion?"

He shrugged, set the cheese aside and pulled a giant skillet from a lower cupboard. "I was looking for a big chunk of land where I could get away from it all. Someplace where I could listen to the grass grow, do some fishing maybe. The Realtor I contacted had a client who wanted to sell a mountain. It worked out perfectly for everyone."

She choked on her coffee. "Perfect for everyone?" she sputtered, not even trying to match his nonchalance.

He looked up from cracking the eggs into a bowl, a single brow raised in question. "What?"

"What? You say that as if you bopped down to the local quick mart to buy a pack of gum. But you bought a whole *mountain*. With an eight-*hundred*-year-old mansion on it. I'd like to see at least a hint of excitement, enthusiasm, *something*."

Another fleeting smile pulled at his lips as he poured the egg mixture into the pan, the hot sizzle filling the room. "At the time I was excited. It was the first thing I'd ever owned. The first house I'd ever lived in."

What? She leaned forward over her cup, her reporter's instinct on full alert. "The first house you'd ever lived in?" she prompted.

He hesitated for a moment, debating, no doubt, whether or not he wanted to answer, but then he nodded. "I grew up an orphan, Ms. Rose. Just like the little boys and girls on the other side of this mountain. My mother was a sixteen-year-old streetwalker from New York City who abandoned me without even looking at me. I hadn't even owned a car before I bought this place."

An orphan.

Her heart ached at the statement. So the accident hadn't been Jason Kent's first clash with life's harsh realities. Well, she'd wondered why the man, an obvious recluse, had opened a group home. Now she knew. But a thousand other questions crowded her brain, where he'd gotten his money foremost among them. She'd assumed he'd been born into it. Old, prolific, stodgy money. But she'd been wrong.

Elation surged through her as she realized what a great story she'd stumbled into. A rags-to-riches tale where the intrepid tycoon still had enough heart, as he sat upon his pile of gold, to build a group home for kids. Add the mountain and the mansion. Her readers were going to love it, providing she got enough facts to write it. She leaned farther forward, her next question pounding to get out.

But before she could ask it, Kent tossed the cheese and mushrooms onto the omelette and then held his hand up to forestall her. "I recognize that rabid reporter's glint in your eye, Ms. Rose. Your magazine sent you up here to write a story on Kent House. I don't want little tidbits about me bleeding into it. No more personal questions, although I'll be happy to answer any you might have about Kent House and the children currently waiting to be adopted."

The children. Her heart twisted in her chest. No, she didn't want to go down that path, but she didn't want Kent to figure out he was the subject of the article, either. Her questions would have to wait.

All but one. A mischievous smile pulled at her lips. "Okay, we'll change the subject. And I'll wait to talk to you about Kent House until I have my paper and pen with me, but I do have one question that has been burning a hole in my brain since last night. And it's not *exactly* personal."

He gave her a wary look as he expertly folded the omelette, cut it in half, slid the halves onto two plates and shoved the plates toward her. "And that question would be?" He took his cane and headed toward the table.

She retrieved the omelettes, along with a couple of forks, set them down on the table and gave Kent a teasing smile as they both dropped into their chairs. "I've got to hear the story behind that room I'm staying in. You planning a visit from Cinderella? A lost princess maybe?"

He grimaced. His expression clearly said that he'd expected her to ask the question sooner or later, and he wasn't thrilled about having to answer it. "It's just a room." He dismissed the question with a negligent wave of his hand and shoved a bite of omelette into his mouth.

She rolled her eyes. "Oh please. You could describe that room a hundred different ways, but none of them would be *just a room.*"

Irritation flickered in his eyes, but he didn't say anything. He just ignored her, cutting another bite from the omelette and forking it into his mouth.

Oh no, he wasn't going to block her out that easily. She had two older brothers. She'd learned early on how to make the reluctant, closemouthed male talk. Challenge their delicate male egos.

She flashed him a wicked, prove-to-me-what-you've-got-big-boy smile. "Come on, Mr. Kent. A room that pink in a bachelor's place has *got* to have an explanation. You can't *possibly* want me to use my imagination to come up with it, do you?" There. Let him ignore *that.*

His sapphire gaze snapped up from his plate and locked onto hers. "You needn't worry about the room, Ms. Rose. I had it decorated for my daughter. When I thought there might be one. There's one just like it next door. Only, for a boy. I thought you'd be more comfortable with frilly pink than shoot-em-up brown."

The blood drained from her face.

A daughter.

And a son.

She dropped her gaze from his and stared at her omelette, her appetite smashed like so many shattered dreams and splintered hopes. His words slashed at her heart, tearing open hidden wounds.

When I thought there might be one.

"Are you all right, Ms. Rose?" Concern sounded in his voice.

"I'm fine." She managed to push the words from her lips and somehow make herself sound fine. But she wasn't. Old pain swamped her like a tidal wave crashing to shore, the waters closing over her head, blocking out the light and the air and threatening to drown her in their wake.

She stared at her plate, aimlessly pushing her omelette from one location to another. She'd been starving when she'd crept through the dark halls to get to the kitchen. But now she just wanted to go back to her room where she could turn off the lights and lie on the bed and let the darkness swallow her up.

Twenty-five.
Twenty-six.
Twenty-seven.
Jason lay flat on the padded bench in the gym, his hands spread wide on the barbell as he pressed it up from his chest again and again and again. Not his favorite pastime. In fact, he hated weights. He'd lifted when he was in the field because brute strength had saved his sorry neck more than once, but running had always been his preference for staying in shape.

But running wasn't an option anymore, and he'd needed something hard and physical to keep his mind off the lovely Ms. Rose. Something to help burn his guilt away.

Thirty.
Thirty-one.
Thirty-two.
It wasn't working. He'd been lifting weights and working on one machine or the other for the last three hours.

Sweat poured off him, and his arms felt like hellfire on Sunday morning. But the guilt was still there. Pushing. Prodding. Nipping at his conscience.

Damn it, she'd just had to know about that blasted room, and she'd had the audacity to challenge his manhood to get her answer.

And he, half-witted moron that he was, had risen to the bait.

With an angry growl he pressed the weight up one more time, the muscles in his arms screaming with fatigue. He should have ignored his affronted manhood and said, why, I love pink. Pink is my favorite color.

But he hadn't. He'd snapped at her instead. And something in what he'd said had upset her. She'd gone pale as a ghost and all but closed herself off from him. Oh, she'd sat there and picked at her omelette with a sad, hollow look in her eyes and pretended to make polite conversation. But she hadn't really eaten a damned bite. And her side of the conversation had consisted of short, lifeless answers and silent nods of her head.

He gritted his teeth and pressed the weight until his arms were extended one more time. He'd stopped by her room at noon with her dry clothes and an invitation for lunch, hoping she'd look better. But she hadn't. And she hadn't accepted his invitation to lunch, either. She'd just taken the clothes and mumbled something about having work to do.

What work, he'd like to know? They hadn't discussed Kent House at all. Not one word. So it's not like she had a lot of information to write down or sort through. Besides, if she was working with that distracted, haunted look in her eyes, he'd eat this damned barbell.

He thrust the weight into the air with a frustrated snarl. He *hated* that haunted look. Hated the fact that he'd put it there. Maybe that's why he wanted to storm up the stairs and demand to know what was bothering her. Demand to know what was bothering her—so he could fix it.

A hideous thought if he'd ever heard one.

What made him think he could fix her problems? He sure as hell couldn't fix his own. Some problems were just too big to be fixed.

And he didn't have any right to be messing in her life anyway. The decision he'd made last night was definitely the best for everyone concerned. He'd stay as far away from her as possible. Whatever problems she had she would have to deal with herself.

Footsteps sounded in the study, catching his attention and sending a shot of adrenaline through him. The lovely Ms. Rose had left her room. He ignored the obvious reason for the excitement coursing through his veins—his predictable male response to a gorgeous woman—and concentrated on the fact that he was glad Ms. Rose had finally wandered downstairs. He didn't like the idea of her sitting up there all alone staring at the walls. He knew how little comfort these cold, gray stones offered.

He lowered the weight to his chest and lay motionless, his ears straining as he listened to the sound of her footsteps. Would she head his way? Or drop onto the sofa and watch the fire? Or maybe she'd go on to another room. She might be looking for him and, not finding him in the study, she might not think to look in the gym. She might not even remember it was there. Maybe he should call out to her?

No. He definitely shouldn't.

Her footsteps stopped momentarily and he held his breath, waiting. The footsteps sounded again, each step getting a little louder.

She was heading his way.

His heart beat faster, pumping a fresh surge of adrenaline through his veins. He heaved the barbell off his chest, slamming it into the rack behind his head. Dropping his feet to either side of the bench, he sat up just as Ms. Rose came through the gym door. The smell of sweet jasmine filled the gym.

She spied him sitting on the bench, gave him a little wave and even managed a fairly convincing smile. "Hi. Thought I'd come looking for company. It's too…quiet up there."

Yes. He knew. He snatched the towel from the end of the bench and wiped the sweat from his eyes. "Done working?"

She frowned in confusion.

He squelched the urge to smile. She wasn't a very good liar. She didn't even remember that's the excuse she'd given him at noon to stay buried in her room. He'd give her a minute. It would come to her.

She'd changed back into her clothes, an occurrence he would have been better off without. Her soft, yellow sweater hugged her breasts with an exuberance that sent his libido soaring, and her stonewashed jeans clung to her feminine curves tightly enough to make a few extra beads of sweat run down his temples. But it wasn't her physical state that concerned him. It was her mental state.

Although a slight tension remained in her face and a few shadows still lurked in her hazel eyes, she certainly looked better than she had at noon. And she was obviously trying to convince him, and possibly herself, that nothing was wrong—a lie it would be safest for both of them to accept.

And it was time to let her off the hook. "When I stopped by with your clothes, you told me you were working. Remember?"

The light dawned in her eyes. "Oh yeah. I'd forgotten. I didn't work very long. I got tired and napped instead."

Uh-huh.

She moved into the gym, letting her gaze slide over the different pieces of equipment. "Pretty fancy gym you have here."

He shrugged. "It serves its purpose."

She looked back at him, her gaze dropping to his arms, still sweaty and pumped up from his workout. Feminine appreciation sparked in her eyes, and a mischievous smile slanted her lips. "I can see that."

Surprise whipped through him, followed by the hard crack of desire. White-hot and demanding. He dropped his hands to his lap, letting the towel hide his arousal. It had been three years since any woman had looked at him with anything other than horror on her face. Three long years. God, he'd forgotten how intoxicating a woman's interest could be.

Ms. Rose's wouldn't last, of course. It would disappear as soon as she looked back at his face. But right now, as her gaze slid over his arms and torso with pure, feminine appreciation he was going to savor every second of it.

Unfortunately, as soon as her gaze hit his left shoulder, recognition flashed in her eyes. Looking up to meet his gaze, she pointed at the tattoo. "You were in Special Forces."

He cocked a brow. "You recognize the tattoo?"

She nodded, excitement shining in her eyes. "My brother, Ryan, has one just like it. He spent four years there. How about you?"

This was the last thing he wanted to talk about. But for the first time since his blunder this morning, the shadows were gone from her eyes. Only interest sparkled there now, and to keep that, he could answer a few questions. "The same."

"Rank?"

"Lieutenant."

"Cool. And then what?"

"More of the same. But in the private sector."

Her gaze flashed back to his left shoulder. She strode toward him, zeroing in on the tattoo that sat just above and to the right of his Special Forces one. The one of the liberty bell with blood dripping from its famous crack.

Surprise flashed across her features. "You were a merc?"

He hated that name. Mercenary implied a man whose skills could be bought by anyone for anything for the right amount of money. The secret, elite force he had worked for hadn't been anything like that. They hired out to only one country, for one objective, for one ideal. But he wasn't going to spend the next three hours explaining that to a woman whose fingers were wrapped tightly around a very public pen. "Yes," he admitted with a growl. "I was a merc."

A single, delicate brow arched high. "Dirty deeds done dirt cheap? My sword to the highest bidder? Or for God and country?"

He gave a humorless laugh. "None of the above. How do you know so much about mercs?"

"I did an article on them about four years ago. Most of the guys I interviewed fell into one of the above categories."

His stomach did a hard roll. Now there was a picture he didn't want to think about. The lovely Ms. Rose with that eager, naive smile, talking to men who slit people's throats for a living. Men she'd probably interviewed alone.

He shook off the cold chill clawing its way up his spine. Since the look on her face now was avid interest instead of revulsion or raw fear she'd obviously made it through the interviews unscathed. But he still didn't like being associated with men who would fit into any of the above categories.

He gave her his blandest look. "And you want to pigeonhole me into one of those lovely categories?"

She flashed him a teasing smile. "Yeah."

He gave his head a sad shake. "Okay then, for God and country." He gave his lips a wry twist. "Providing they could afford us."

Now the lights in her eyes almost exploded. "Us?"

Oh yeah, he'd bet she would just love to know about the private little agency he had worked for. But some questions he couldn't answer, even if doing so would keep that light in her eyes. "Move on, Ms. Rose."

She wrinkled her nose at him. "All right. But at least tell me this. Is that where you made your money for this little getaway and Kent House? As a high-priced gun?"

The woman was a bottomless pit of nosy questions. "Yes. That and the stock market."

One of those lovely brows winged upward again. "The stock market? A merc with a couple of pens and a plastic pocket protector sticking out of his fatigues? Now there's an interesting picture."

He gave her a disparaging look. "Isn't it though?"

She chuckled at his dry answer, but then her look turned serious and she tipped her head toward his leg. The one he supported with his cane. "Is that where you got hurt?"

His gut clenched, but he managed to push the answer past his lips. "Yes."

She hesitated for just a moment as if trying to decide

whether or not to ask her next question. "Do you mind if I ask what happened?"

He minded. But he'd answer. Because he didn't want her to *know* he minded. And because he wanted to keep her here, where he could smell her and watch her and talk to her.

He managed to shrug as if the retelling of the worst five minutes of his life didn't mean a damned thing. "Bad luck and worse timing. I was blowing a bridge in South America, trying to keep the local gunrunners from using it to transport illegal weapons, when one of the arms runners popped out of the jungle. Needless to say he wasn't very happy that I was about to put a giant dent in his yearly income. Unfortunately, I'd already lit the fuse."

Ms. Rose gasped softly, but she didn't say anything, she just waited silently for him to continue.

"Luckily, I managed to put him down before he separated my head from my shoulders with the rusty machete he was wielding. But I wasn't quick enough to avoid this." He touched his cheek. "Or get away from the bridge before the blast went off." Despite his efforts to keep it out, bitterness edged his last words.

Sadness filled the lovely Ms. Rose's eyes as she met his gaze. "I'm sorry."

Pity. The last thing he wanted from her. "Don't be. Injuries are part of the game." But he wasn't going to talk about the game and its ugliness anymore. It was depressing both of them. "My turn to ask the questions. You said you had one brother. Any other siblings?"

Thankfully, she accepted the change of subject with an easy grace and an easier smile. "I have a younger sister and one more brother."

"The brother older? Or younger?"

She rolled her eyes. "Both the boys are older, curse the fates."

He smiled at her impatience. "Were they tough on you?"

"Not tough really. Just..." Her lips twitched wryly. "Inconvenient sometimes."

He cocked a brow, inviting her to elaborate.

"Well, you know, when you're in grade school it's great to have two older brothers chase the bullies away on the playground. But when you hit high school and start dating, it's a whole other story."

He chuckled softly. "I imagine it is. What about now? They still pick on your boyfriends?" The question was out of his mouth before he'd given it any real thought.

She flicked her wrist, waving off the question as if it had no significance. "No need. I've sworn off men." She chuckled then, trying to sound as if the question had amused her. But the laugh was a little forced. A little over-bright. And the look in her eyes was a little desperate.

If she'd made that decision, he didn't think she'd made it easily. He narrowed his eyes on her, trying to look deeper into her mind. "Really?"

Like thieves in the night the shadows stole back into her eyes and they took on that sad, haunted look again. "Really." Her voice was as flat as the Kuwaiti desert.

His stomach clenched. "Damn. I did it again, didn't I?"

She looked back at him, her expression as distracted as it had been this morning. "What?"

"Said something I shouldn't have."

"Oh no." She shook her head. "I'm fine, really. I just seem to be in a funny mood today."

She looked around the gym as if she were trying to find something to do. Finally, she faced him again. "Listen,

I'm going back to my room. Work a little. I didn't get much done this morning, so I should probably get busy.''

No way. He wasn't going to let her wander off and start brooding again. He glanced at his watch. ''Wait a minute. I have a better idea. You've hardly eaten all day. You have to be starving. And after spending the last three hours in here, I certainly am. Can I talk you into fixing us an early dinner?'' A little rude, he supposed, to ask her to cook when she was his guest. But she needed something to derail her thoughts, and it was the only thing he could come up with on short notice.

When she didn't answer, just stood there looking a bit lost, he gave her a teasing smile and a little nudge. ''I'll settle for peanut butter and jelly.''

That got a laugh out of her. ''All right, I'll cook. But if I have access to that fancy kitchen and all that good food, it won't be peanut-butter-and-jelly sandwiches.''

He gave an exaggerated sigh of relief. ''Thank God. I didn't even like those things as a kid.'' He tipped his head toward the door. ''Why don't you go on. I'll shower and join you there.''

With a nod and wave she headed out of the gym.

He watched her go. Watched the door shut behind her. And then he crushed the towel in his hands with a savage growl. He was an *idiot*. He should have just let her wander off. Then he wouldn't have to think about her. Wouldn't have to look at those sad hazel eyes. Wouldn't have to smell the sweet scent of jasmine every time she walked by him.

He already knew that every room, every hall he'd seen her in would seem ten times as empty when she left. A hundred times as lonely. A thousand times more like hell on earth. And right now she was just a woman who'd gotten lost and ended up on his doorstep. A woman he knew almost nothing about.

Except, of course, that she had two brothers that had championed her on the playground and years later stood around in the driveway waiting for her dates to drop her off. That she smelled like sweet jasmine. And liked to cook.

He gritted his teeth and stared up at the flat stone ceiling above his head. He was already in trouble up to his eyeballs.

But he couldn't just banish her to fight her demons alone. He couldn't. And if that meant his own loneliness and madness would loom that much closer when she left, so be it.

Chapter Four

Jason hurried down the dim hall toward the kitchen as quickly as his leg and cane would allow. His hair was still wet, but the short military cut would dry quickly and he hadn't wanted to leave Ms. Rose alone any longer than he already had.

A pathetic excuse if he'd ever heard one.

Granted, he wanted to cheer Ms. Rose up, and he didn't want her alone in the kitchen any longer than necessary. But that's not why he'd rushed his shower and skipped drying his hair. He'd hurried because the idea of sharing a meal with a beautiful woman made his heart pound and his palms sweat and his libido kick into overdrive—all dangerous indications that he was losing touch with reality.

Wanting to cheer Ms. Rose up was one thing. Letting himself get carried away by the situation was quite another. Ms. Rose might have looked at him in the gym for one brief moment like he was a man and not a monster. But the bottom line was that, for all intents and purposes, he was a monster.

And she was just a reporter stranded here by the storm. A reporter who would be gone as soon as the storm was over. She probably couldn't *wait* to put this place—and him—behind her. Facts he'd do well to remember.

As he got closer to the kitchen, enticing smells spilled into the hall. He drew in a deep breath, savoring not only the mouth-watering aromas but the singular pleasure that someone else was creating them. For this moment he was not alone in this oppressive pile of stones.

Taking another greedy whiff, he pushed into the kitchen. "Smells great."

Ms. Rose jerked her head up from the stove, her eyes wide, her mouth round with a startled "Oh."

"Sorry, I didn't mean to sneak up on you."

She pulled herself together and shook her head. "Don't worry about it. I was just lost in thought."

Which is exactly what he didn't want. He'd come up with this dinner idea so she wouldn't have to think about whatever was bothering her. He tipped his head toward the skillet on the stove. "What did you decide to cook?"

She gave him a distracted smile. "How do you feel about Thai food?"

His mouth was watering just thinking about it. He couldn't remember the last time a meal had consisted of more than something he could throw together in five minutes or less. "Love it. Anything specific in mind?"

"Chicken with peanut sauce?" she suggested hopefully.

"Oh yeah. What can I do to help?" He didn't even try to hide his pleasure at the prospect of a real meal.

She chuckled softly. "You sound a little over-eager,

Mr. Kent. When was the last time you had something fancier than an omelette or a hamburger?''

He liked the sound of her quiet laughter. It was a little hesitant and tension still radiated from the corners of her eyes, but the small chuckle was a step in the right direction. He gave her a smile, trying to get her to relax even more. "Too damned long ago. So I repeat, what can I do to help?"

She glanced at the stove where the chicken was sizzling away in a large skillet and rice was steaming in a pot next to it. "Actually, everything's under control. Once the chicken's browned the only thing left to do is dump the sauce ingredients into the pan and let them simmer. Guess you're going to have to just sit and keep me company while the chicken cooks.''

Anytime. "How about a glass of wine while you work? I have a great wine cellar." And a glass of wine might go a long way toward helping her relax and getting her to let go of whatever was bothering her.

She picked up a fork and started turning the chicken, a small grin pulling at her lips. "I'll bet you do. Right next to the dungeon, right?"

He laughed. "Actually, as much as I hate to disappoint you, there is no dungeon. Just a musty old basement filled with old trunks and old furniture and old cobwebs."

She cocked a brow, a hint of mischief sparkling in her hazel eyes. "No implements of torture? No rat-infested cells? No dusty, old skeletons?"

Yeah, a little easy conversation, a little bit of wine, he'd have those shadows gone from her eyes in no time. He shook his head. "Sorry, not a one."

She gave a dramatic sigh. "How disappointing."

He smiled. "Isn't it though? My wine cellar, on the

other hand, would never let you down. Name your favorite, chances are I have a bottle on hand.''

She finished turning the last piece of chicken. ''I don't have a favorite. You pick.''

''You must have some preference. White, red? Sweet, dry? Domestic, imported?''

A slight flush tinged her cheeks. ''I hate to tell you this, particularly since you're so proud of your wine cellar, but I don't know anything about wine. I'm a Pepsi drinker. But if you have a favorite bottle of something, I'd love to try that. As long as it's not expensive,'' she amended. ''I wouldn't know a bottle of expensive wine from a bottle of Boone's Farm, so don't waste anything really good on me.''

Waste? Never. It had been over three years since he'd shared a good bottle of wine with a beautiful woman. ''I'll be right back.''

He left the kitchen and headed down the hall. The wine ''cellar'' was the last room on the right. In this mansion one didn't need to descend to the basement to get a cool, dark room, and keeping the wine cellar close to the kitchen had seemed a practical choice when he moved in.

He pushed open the door and moved into the chamber. He knew just the bottle he wanted. He quickly located it and wiped it clean of dust. Ms. Rose might not know the difference between one wine and the other, but after tonight, she would definitely know the difference between a mediocre wine and a great one.

Pushing back into the kitchen, he held the bottle up for her perusal. ''Light and sweet.'' And expensive. Very, very expensive. But he wouldn't tell her that. ''Perfect for an adventurous Pepsi drinker.''

She glanced up from moving the chicken from the skillet to a plate. "Great. I took two glasses out." She pointed to two crystal glasses sitting out on the counter.

"Perfect."

While he joined her at the counter and started uncorking the wine, she removed the rest of the chicken and dumped a plateful of chopped onions into the skillet.

He looked into the pan and then back to her, raising a brow. "I thought you didn't like onions?"

She gave him a questioning look.

"You didn't want them in your omelette, remember?"

She laughed softly. "Oh well, onions don't belong in omelettes. They overpower the cheese and eggs. But in peanut sauce…they're a must."

"Ah." He pulled the cork from the wine and began pouring the golden liquid into the waiting glasses.

The soft glug of the wine accompanied the sizzle of the onions. It was a domestic sound accompanied by a domestic scene—a man and a woman standing together at a counter fixing dinner. He imagined it was a scene that took place in thousands of homes all over the world every day. He imagined most people didn't give it a second thought.

But he thought about it. How nice it was to share a simple chore like fixing a meal. How nice it was to have a woman in his house. To smell the sweet scent of jasmine drifting through the sharper aroma of onions. Oh yeah, he thought about it. More than he should for a man who would find himself alone when this storm blew past.

He looked back at Ms. Rose. She was busily stirring the onions in the pan, keeping them from burning. "Sure you don't need any help?"

She shook her head. "Once these onions are done— and they're fast approaching—I just pour the rest of the

ingredients into the pan, add the chicken and let it simmer
for twenty minutes."

"Good, we can sit and enjoy the wine while it cooks."

"Sounds good."

He moved himself and the wine to the table.

Apparently deciding that the onions were done, she
dumped the rest of the ingredients into the pan and joined
him at the table, dropping into her chair and reaching for
her glass. She slowly spun the glass in front of her, the
crystal humming softly as its base scraped against the table's surface. "Pretty."

The cut glass of the Waterford crystal caught the light
and mixed it with the rich, golden color of the wine. The
effect was brilliant and dazzling, but it was the woman
who held his attention.

He drew in a slow, deep breath, relishing her sweet
scent and trying to concentrate on the conversation. "Try
it. It tastes even better than it looks."

She brought the glass to her lips and took a tentative
sip. Her hazel eyes widened with surprised delight. "Oh,
this is good."

Almost as good as watching the pleasure on her face.
"Glad you like it."

He took a sip from his own glass. There were a million
questions he wanted to ask her. What had put the shadows
in her eyes? Why had she given up men? And why, if
she'd made that decision, did it make her so unhappy?
But asking any of those questions would only make the
shadows in her eyes darker, and he was trying to chase
them away. So he'd keep the conversation light and easy.
"You told me about your brothers earlier. How about
your sister? What's she like?"

"Irene's the baby of the family, so we like to tell her
she's spoiled rotten. But she's not. She's a sweetie." She

took another sip of wine, but she didn't swallow it immediately. She closed her eyes, tipped her head and parted her lips slightly, letting the liquid run over her tongue as she savored the sweetness. Sensuous delight played across her features. "Mmm. I definitely like this."

Heat flowed through his veins. Sweet ecstasy. There had been a time when he could put that look on a woman's face. But those days were over. Now, this was as close as he'd probably ever come to seeing that expression again. He drank in the sight like a bedouin quenching his thirst at an oasis.

She took another sip, savoring it the same way, those beautiful bee-stung lips parting softly, her eyelids slipping to half-mast.

Oh man, she was going to kill him. He cleared his throat. "So tell me, Ms. Rose, who did you get along with better? Your sister or your brothers?" A lame question if he'd ever heard one. But he'd been lucky to come up with that.

She took one more sip, a quick one this time, and set the glass back on the table, the crystal chiming softly as it hit the hard surface. She gave him a teasing smile. "You know, Mr. Kent, every time you say 'Ms. Rose' I want to look around for my mother. Couldn't you please call me Angie?"

Angie. Common sense screamed at him not to do it. Not to cross that line of familiarity. But even as he thought it, his tongue formed the name. "Angie, I think we can get rid of the 'Mr. Kent' too. Call me Jason." *Fool.* Now he'd really done it. "So who'd you get along with better?"

"Definitely my sister. We had to join forces against the boys, or they would have overrun the house."

He smiled at that, remembering his own youth. "Yeah,

when I was in the orphanage, the boys were always trying to lord it over the girls.''

She took another sip of wine, giving him a knowing look over the glass brim. ''I'll bet you did. Did the girls fight back?''

''Absolutely. Like an army of crazed ants. They were merciless.''

She leaned back in her chair, laughing. ''Did they use the old spray-the-boys-with-toilet-water trick just before they went out to play with all the other little boys?''

He gave her a surprised look. ''Yeah, they did. How'd you know that?''

She chuckled softly, sipping at her wine. ''It's a universal girl thing. You want to get even with a boy but you don't want to work too hard at it, so you spray him with toilet water and let every boy within whiffing distance razz him for you. Perfect revenge.''

The wine was relaxing her, the conversation putting a sparkle in her eyes. Good. ''Very sneaky. Any little boys you pulled that on get even?'' He gave her a cocky smile. ''Put snakes in your bed?''

Her eyes popped wide. ''Yeah. Ryan did, the little rat. And not just one. He found a whole nest of babies and put *those* in my bed. There must have been a dozen of them. When I pulled the covers down they slithered in every direction.'' She clenched her fists and shivered, but she was laughing while she did it. And then her smile turned downright devilish. ''But I got even.''

He gave a mock groan, enjoying her laughter. ''What did you do?''

She gave an evil laugh. ''Honey and peanut butter in his baseball cleats. One hour before a playoff game.''

He winced at the thought of having to play an entire

playoff game in gooey, sticky shoes. "Now *that* is mean."

"Nope, that's what we call *sweet* revenge." She dissolved into laughter, her eyes sparkling with mischief.

God, she was beautiful. Bright. Shining. *Alive.*

And he wanted her.

He wanted to stand up, pull her into his arms and kiss her until neither one of them could breathe. Kiss her until not so much as a hint of shadow lurked in her eyes. Until he remembered what it felt like to be totally, undeniably alive.

There had been a time before the bridge when he would have followed that gut instinct, but he fought it now. Any such move on his part would only frighten the lovely Angie Rose, not comfort her. She might be able to handle his countenance when he was safely ensconced on the other side of the table and his overtures were nothing more than that of a friendly host trying to make his guest comfortable. But he had no doubt that any overtures he might make as a man to a woman would send her scurrying.

And that's what kept him in his chair. The thought of the horror and revulsion that would chase the pleasure from her face. Regret, cold and bitter, settled in his gut. If only his arm had been quicker than his attacker's blade. If only the bomb had waited ten more seconds before it had gone off.

If only.

A fool's prayer. One he'd given up long ago.

Across the table Angie's laughter wound down. She drew a deep, calming breath. "Oh geez, I think I needed that." She caught his gaze. "Thanks."

"Any time." He took a sip of the sweet wine, wishing for the sharp burn of hard whisky. "Any time."

* * *

The next morning Angie leaned against the door frame of the bedroom next to hers and stared into the little boy's room. Shoot-em-up brown all right, complete with a comforter covered in a cowboy-and-Indian motif and a throw rug shaped like a giant cowboy boot patiently waiting at the side of the bed for the patter of little feet.

Sadness pulled at her heart, but it was manageable today. Yesterday it had almost buried her. She shook her head. She thought she'd given up wallowing in that black pit of pain and loss five years ago. Wishful thinking apparently. This whole group home story seemed to have torn open those old wounds with frightening ease. But she wasn't going to let herself get caught in that pain again. It would suck the life right out of her. Five years ago she'd consciously decided not to let that happen. She wasn't going to change her mind now.

Granted, the life she had today wasn't the one she had hoped for when she'd been young and naïve and whole. It certainly wasn't the one she had dreamed of. But it was what she had. And it wasn't all that bad. She was a good reporter. A damned good reporter. And if that's all she was, well, at least she had that.

But what about Jason? She'd been so caught up in her own pain yesterday she hadn't thought about his. But looking at this room, remembering the bitterness in his voice when he'd told her about the bomb blast that had damaged his leg, she knew he'd been hurting, too. And yet, he'd set his own pain aside to cajole her out of her misery last night.

And what did that make him?

Someone she wanted to know better. And she wasn't sure that was such a good thing. If she was interested in him only as a reporter it would be fine, but she suspected she was just as interested in him as a woman. Last night at dinner the wine had relaxed her, but it had been the man who had made her laugh. The man who had made her feel comforted and cared for. Yes, the woman in her definitely wanted to know him better, this retired soldier with his scar and limp, anger and frustration, altruism and compassion.

Not a good thing. She'd given up men. And if she was smart, she'd wait out this storm, staying as far away from the intriguing Jason Kent as she could. Unfortunately, that wasn't an option. She had a story to write and not much time in which to do it.

She glanced out the floor-to-ceiling window across the room. Snow still fell steadily from the skies, but according to the weathermen the storm would move on by tonight. Jason had said it would take a few days for the plows to make it up his road, but she couldn't count on that. Today might be the last day she had here. She couldn't afford to waste it.

She pushed away from the door frame, pulled the door closed on the wild, wild West and headed downstairs to look for Jason, meticulously ignoring the tingle of purely feminine anticipation shimmering through her.

She checked the study first, her heart pounding a little harder than the quick trip down the stairs warranted. A toasty fire burned in the hearth, but Jason wasn't anywhere to be seen, nor did a quick check in the gym turn him up.

Disappointed but undeterred, she went back to the giant foyer and looked around at the doors and halls that led off the cavernous room. She knew where very few of them led so she picked a door at random, twisted the tarnished brass knob and pushed.

Empty. Totally empty with the exception of her long

shadow, the dust on the floor and the cobwebs hanging from the ceiling. With a little shudder she pulled the door shut and moved onto the next one. She pushed open the door and peeked in.

Jason was sitting in the middle of the room in front of a curved counter filled with computers.

"Aha. There you are." Her spirits picking up considerably, she pushed the door wide and stepped into the room.

Jason finished typing something on a keyboard and then glanced over his shoulder at her. "Finally up?"

She nodded, looking around at the rest of the room. With the exception of the semicircular counter curving around Jason, the chamber was empty. No extra furniture sat around, no art hung from the walls, no rugs covered the bare stone floors. Apparently, he didn't like any distractions when he worked.

He swiveled around in his chair to face her. "Hungry? I could fix you something, or there's cereal and fruit if you want to get it yourself."

She shook her head and waved off the offer. "No thanks, I'll be fine until lunch." She stepped into the room, pushing the door shut behind her.

To her surprise the room went almost dark as she did so. She hadn't noticed until now that the room was windowless. If not for the one, two, three...*seven* computers flickering behind Jason they would have been in complete darkness.

She looked at Jason, lifting a brow. "No creature comforts. No aesthetic appointments. No light. The Spartans' approach to the modern-day workplace?"

A hint of a smile pulled at his lips. "Actually, this is the most beautiful room in the mansion. You just can't see it."

"Beautiful, huh?" Maybe she'd missed something. She looked around the room again. It was round, or octagonal to be exact. An interesting shape certainly, with its eight, short, angled walls. But beautiful? She looked back to him. "It just seems...dark to me."

He chuckled softly and pointed behind his computers. "Go look closer."

She wandered beyond the computers toward the far walls. As she got closer, she realized that a fine tracing covered the stones. She looked harder, trying to discern whether the stone had been carved or painted or what. She stumbled to an astonished halt.

"Oh my Lord." She reached out and lightly ran her fingers over the thin strips of lead, the small panes of cool glass. She turned back to Jason. "They're stained glass windows."

He gave her a single, succinct nod, a knowing smile turning his lips.

She turned back to the windows and peered up into the darkness, trying to discern form from shadow. "How tall are they?"

"Twenty feet. Give or take an inch or two."

"Oh geez." Twenty feet high, an easy six feet across, they would be breathtaking with the light streaming through them. She strode back to Jason, facing him from the other side of the computer counter. "Why can't I see them? What's blocking the light?"

"Shutters. Drescher didn't want the winds that howl across these mountains to break the windows, so he had heavy shutters installed when they reconstructed the mansion here. I always closed them before I left on missions." He cast an angry glance at his leg. "After my last assignment, climbing up to reopen them wasn't an option."

Though he tried to keep his tone normal, she could hear the frustration in the last sentence.

And how frustrating it must be to have such beauty so close and not be able to enjoy it. "How long ago was that?"

"Three years."

He'd been putting up with this darkness for *three years?* Way too long. "Why don't you light the room? The colors wouldn't be as brilliant, but at least you could see the windows."

He gave a disgusted huff. "A cheap imitation of the real thing? No thanks. It would hardly be the same."

No, it wouldn't be the same. But it would be something, which was more than he had now in this dark pit of shadow and flickering light. However, he didn't look in the mood for compromise. Time to change the subject. She waved a hand toward the curved counter. "So tell me what you do with all these computers."

His expression eased somewhat as he switched his attention to the monitors. "This morning I'm trading."

She raised her brows in surprise. "Day trading?"

He nodded and looked to the flashing screens.

She peered at him from over the computer tops. "Last night you said you'd made a lot of your money on the stock market. Is that what you meant? Day trading?" She couldn't keep the disbelief from her voice. She didn't know a lot about the stock market. Actually, she knew nothing about the stock market, but what she'd heard about day trading made it sound as risky as trying to earn your money in a casino.

He shook his head. "No, when I was busy making my fortune I would never have risked it on something this volatile. Back then I stuck to the standard stock market. I still do mostly. I just do this—" he waved his hand

toward the screens, a dark smile pulling at his lips
"—when I need something stronger than my own morose
humors to occupy my thoughts."

She wondered why he needed such a diversion today,
but since she'd already brought up unpleasant memories
asking about the windows, she didn't prod. Instead, she
rested her arms on top of one of the monitors and leaned
over to peek at the illuminated screens. "Are you buying
or selling?"

His brows knit as he studied the monitor in front of
him. A single brow shot upward as if he was surprised at
something that had happened on the screen. "Good question." He narrowed his attention to the machine in front
of him.

Something must be happening. His expression was
sharp, intent as he studied the screen. She stood quietly,
watching him. It amazed her how much sheer power he
exuded just sitting in front of a flickering monitor. He
didn't look like some fancy Wall Street executive who
wore expensive Italian suits and had his nails buffed on
Fridays. He looked like a warrior standing on the verge
of battle with those broad shoulders and that hard, take-
no-prisoners expression.

Her heart tripped in her chest. The man exuded strength
and power and pure sexual magnetism. God, he was gorgeous.

Her thoughts stuttered to a halt. Gorgeous? Two days
ago she'd thought his disfigured face would fit nicely in
a horror movie.

She had been so wrong. The scar didn't ruin his handsome face. It saved him from being a pretty boy and
marked him as a man of courage and virility and
strength—traits she knew he possessed after hearing his
story of bombs and bridges and brigands. And right now,

with the left brow raised high, catching the end of his scar and carrying it up into a rakish, sardonic expression, he was sexy. Undeniably, mind-blowingly sexy.

In a flurry of activity, Jason's fingers suddenly flew over the keyboard in front of him. "Selling."

She snapped out of her reverie. "What?"

He glanced at her. "You asked if I was buying or selling."

"Oh yeah." She pushed away from the computer she'd been leaning on. It was suddenly too hot in this small room. Hot and…intimate in the flickering light.

She paced restlessly, trying to draw in a steadying breath. She might find him the sexiest man on earth, but she didn't have a damned thing to offer him, and wishing she did wouldn't make it so.

She ignored the useless pitter-patter of her heart and concentrated on the reason she'd come here. Her story. She waved a hand toward the computers. "You like it? Day trading?"

"I like the mental aerobics of it, yes." He watched her as she paced back and forth, his sapphire gaze intent as he tracked her every move.

She didn't like the close scrutiny. It made her feel nervous, threatened, as if he were trying to see into her soul. She'd give him something else to think about. She cocked a challenging brow. "You just like the mental aerobics? Not the money?"

He shrugged. "I have more money than I can spend in a lifetime and no heirs to spend what's left. Why would I need more money?"

"Some people never have enough."

"I'm not some people."

"But you still do the trading?"

"Strictly for diversion. I don't care if I make money or lose it." His gaze never wavered.

He was telling the truth. He didn't care if he won or lost so long as he kept boredom at bay. An interesting attitude. "Which do you do more of? Win or lose?"

He gave a cynical laugh. "Win. I was always good at playing the market but, now that I don't care if I win or lose, it's as if I have the Midas touch. Everything I touch turns to gold."

She cocked her head and studied him. Was that a hint of poor-little-rich-boy whining she heard? "If you're so bored, why don't you go to work for some big company? There are thousands of corporations that would just love to have someone with a Midas touch managing their funds."

His black scowl returned. "Get serious. No company wants this face wandering down their halls."

She definitely didn't agree. She'd like to see it wandering down her hall at the magazine any day. And she suspected most women would agree wholeheartedly, once they got to know him. But she doubted that he was in the mood to believe her. "If corporate America doesn't appeal to you, why not try something else? There are a million jobs out there. You don't have to sit in this house and brood for the next eighty years."

His scowl got blacker. "What would you suggest I do, Ms. Rose? The only thing I'm trained for is murder and mayhem and, thanks to this leg, those days are over. Now if you'll excuse me I have other business to attend to." Without another word he pushed to his feet and headed out of the office.

She stifled a defeated sigh as she watched him walk out of the room, his cane tapping an even rhythm on the stone floors. Back to "Ms. Rose," were they? She walked around the computers and dropped into Jason's chair, the residual heat from his body soaking into hers as he pulled the door shut behind him. She'd gotten a little more information for her article, but not nearly as much as she'd hoped to.

She leaned back in his chair, letting the wavering light wrap around her, listening to the tap of his cane fade as he disappeared into the mansion. She supposed she should feel bad for upsetting him, but she couldn't muster any sympathy. The man was feeling plenty sorry for himself. And if he was burying himself in this mansion because he thought his leg and scar made him ineffective he was the biggest fool to ever draw air.

She shook her head, frustration running through her. Self-pity. It was a deep, soul-eating pit that would swallow him up if he let it. Unfortunately, she knew from experience that the only one who could pull Jason out of that sticky morass was Jason.

Which did not mean she had to stand by and let him drown in his discontent. There was no reason why she couldn't give him a subtle reminder that the world was still out here, waiting for him to join it. Just a little nudge to encourage him to climb out of that hellish pit.

And she knew just what that little nudge should be. She smiled into the darkness and swiveled the chair around until she faced the dark, stained glass windows.

Perfect.

Chapter Five

Jason stood in front of the floor-to-ceiling window in his bedroom, staring out at the blinding landscape. The storm had blown through during the night, leaving behind three feet of snow and bright sunshine. The resulting panorama was one any artist would kill for.

Pristine. Sparkling. New.

And this morning he hated it.

It reminded him that the one thing he would never be again was sparkling and new, and he didn't need any more reminders. The lovely Angie Rose reminded him every time she walked into a room, which was why he'd spent most of yesterday in this room trying to avoid the woman and all of last night standing right here, watching the storm blow itself out.

As the final winds had raged across the mountains, old issues had raged inside his head, issues he had thought he'd made peace with. Issues he *had* made peace with, damn it. Until Angie Rose had stumbled into his life. Now every time he saw her, every time the scent of jasmine teased his senses, he ached for the future he'd dreamed of and worked for and planned for.

A future he was never going to have.

Ms. Rose might think he didn't have to sit in this mansion and brood for the next eighty years, but she didn't have a clue. No company was going to hire someone who looked like him.

He clenched his fists in angry frustration and, for the thousandth time in the last eighteen hours, tried to shove that insidious thought from his head. What the *hell* did he care if someone hired him or not? He didn't need a damned job. He had more money than he'd spend in any one lifetime. Any ten lifetimes.

But even as he made the adamant mental statement another thought echoed in his head. And no matter how much he objected or how hard he tried to ignore it the thought would not go away. He did care. Because it wasn't about needing the money a job would produce. It was about purpose. A man needed purpose in life. And he didn't have one.

Before the bridge he'd had all kinds of purpose. Save the world. Free the oppressed. And most important, make enough money as a merc to retire at thirty-five and spend the rest of his life as a husband and father.

His heart caught in his chest. A husband and father. It was all he'd ever dreamed of growing up. All any orphan ever dreamed of. Family. But there wouldn't be any family now.

The only way he'd ever convince a woman to get within two feet of him would be to entice her with his money. And he wasn't interested in paying some woman to pretend she could stand the sight of him, or to fake her passion for him, either. He wanted the real thing or nothing at all.

He laughed humorlessly, the hollow sound echoing off his bedroom walls. Nothing at all. That's exactly what he had. A fact he was ruthlessly reminded of every second he was in Ms. Rose's presence.

He scrubbed a hand down his face. Forget it. He could stand here and brood for the next millennium and it wouldn't change a damned thing. A bottle of good whisky, on the other hand, might well deliver oblivion. He snatched up his cane and headed for his study, where he could scare up a roaring fire and a bottle of Crown Royal.

He was halfway down the stairs when the front door flew open and Ms. Rose all but skipped into the foyer from outside, her hair flying free around her head, her cheeks rosy from the cold and her eyes sparkling with excitement.

Beautiful and glowing and vibrantly alive.

Everything he wasn't prepared to face this morning. He gritted his teeth and froze on the stairs. With any luck she'd blow by without even noticing him.

Perversely, she spotted him immediately, those bright hazel eyes homing in on him. "Have you looked outside? It's *gorgeous* out there."

"What's so gorgeous about three feet of snow?" His voice was as rough and short-tempered as his mood.

She halted in her tracks and gave him a quick once-over, her gaze zeroing in on the beard stubble he hadn't bothered to shave. "Bad night?"

He raised a single, sardonic brow. "What makes you think so?"

She wrinkled her nose at his sarcasm. "That bad, huh?"

Worse. And he had no intention of prolonging it. He had a bottle of whisky waiting for him. "Did you want something, Ms. Rose?"

She winced at his formal address. "You're not going to start that again are you?"

Absolutely. He wasn't prepared to cross that line of familiarity today. It was too much of a tease. Too much of an illusion of normality when there was none. He stared silently back at her.

She gave her head a short shake and rolled her eyes. "Oh, fine. Have it your way. But yes, I want something. I have a surprise for you."

Alarm raised the hairs on the back of his neck. "Surprise?" The last surprise he'd had in his life had been her, standing on his porch. He wasn't sure he could take another one.

"Yeah. A surprise. Come on."

Self-preservation kept his feet firmly rooted to the stair. She narrowed her eyes. "What? Are you just going to stand there all day?"

"Maybe."

She tsked testily and waved him adamantly down the stairs. "Come on. It's just a little surprise. It won't bite and it won't kill you."

He wouldn't bet on it. Just being in her presence was sheer torture, but she obviously wouldn't be deterred so he stepped down the stairs and joined her in the foyer.

She smiled brilliantly and started unwinding the winter scarf wrapped around her neck. "Okay, hold on, I've got to blindfold you."

He gave her a quelling look. "I don't think that'll be necessary."

She flashed him a flirty little pixie smile full of shiny teeth and eager anticipation. "Don't be such a spoilsport, you're going to like the surprise. I promise.'' She drew a small cross over her heart and shamelessly batted her lashes.

He shook his head. The woman was too damned determined for her own good. And too damned cute for his. He heaved a disparaging sigh and tipped his head down so she could easily reach it.

She stepped close, arranging the scarf in her hands as she prepared to wind it around his head. The cold still clinging to her chilled his skin. Her scent teased his senses. The storm and sweet jasmine. Lord help him, the promise of heaven from the depths of hell.

He closed his eyes against the sharp stab of longing and allowed her to wrap the scarf around his head. His fingers tightened around the top of his cane until the wings of the eagle bit painfully into his flesh. Five more minutes. And then he could escape to his study where he could lock the door and drain that bottle of whisky.

She gave the knot behind his head one final tug. ''Okay, follow me.'' She clamped her hand around his arm and gently tugged him forward.

''Where are we going?''

She chuckled softly. ''Now that would ruin the surprise.''

She led him around in a circle for a few minutes, to confuse him he presumed, then she opened a door and led him through. He recognized the smell of plastic and working circuits immediately. They were in his office.

She quickly untied the knot and whipped the blindfold from his eyes. ''Ta-da!''

Colored light, rich and vibrant, exploded around him. Greens and golds, reds and purples, blues and impossibly pure yellows flooded the room. The shutters were open.

Elation surged through him. The brilliant sunshine

poured through the stained glass like water through precious gems. He drank in the luminous, dancing light and
stared with unabashed pleasure at the giant pictures de-
picting individual stories from the Bible. He'd forgotten
how beautiful the windows and the extraordinary light
show they created were.

So beautiful…and for him, absolutely inaccessible.

Humiliation poured over him like scalding lava, searing
the joy out of him. He felt like a little boy who couldn't
manage to put his Tinkertoy house together so his teacher
had stepped in and done it for him. He closed his eyes,
blocking out the color and the windows and the light. But
he couldn't block out the shame.

How had he ever come to this? Three years ago he'd
been the person who rushed in to fix other people's problems. The big bad soldier who, against sometimes impossible odds, stole into the enemy camp to save the hostage
or chase away the bad guys. Now he was so helpless a
tiny slip of a girl had to open his own windows for him.

His face burned. Why hadn't that damned bomb done
its work three years ago and blown him to pieces? Death
would have been far preferable to this undignified existence that chafed at him like a hair shirt. Anger roiled in
his gut. Anger at the fates and anger at Ms. Rose.

Holding onto his control by the barest of threads he
turned to her. "Are you in the habit of rearranging other
people's homes to suit yourself, Ms. Rose?" He kept his
tone as cool as the subzero temperatures outside.

Her eyes widened at his attack. "I wasn't opening the
windows for me. I thought you'd like it," she defended
herself.

That was the trouble with Pollyannas. They thought a
happy smile and a cheery attitude would make everyone's
troubles go away. But nothing was going to give him back

the full use of his leg. Nothing. And the last thing he needed was this Pollyanna throwing the fact in his scarred face.

The control on his anger slipped completely. "You thought I'd *like* being shown just how useless I am?"

She fell back a step, her eyes opening even wider. "I wasn't trying to do anything of the kind." Indignation filled her.

"Really? Was it hard to open those shutters, Ms. Rose?"

Her eyes narrowed to thin hazel bands, as if she knew exactly where his question was leading. To her credit she didn't back away from either his anger or the truth. She tipped her chin up and met his gaze head on. "No. As I'm sure you're aware, Drescher designed the system brilliantly. With the metal rungs going up the outside walls for easy access and the sliding track system on the shutters themselves, opening them was easy."

"But I couldn't do it."

The line of her lips hardened, but her gaze never wavered. "No, you couldn't."

The words hung between them, naked and unadorned.

Resentment sparkled in her eyes. "Do you feel better now that I've said it?"

"Yes," he snapped.

"Liar. You're sad and frustrated and angry. And you figure if you can make me feel just as bad, you'll somehow feel better. But I won't be bullied, Jason. And I won't apologize for opening the windows, either. It's not my fault you got hurt on the battlefield."

She held her hands up to forestall his comment. "I know, it wasn't your fault, either. But this is what you have now." She swept her hand toward his leg. "It's time to make peace with it and move forward."

His anger tightened to a hard, icy knot in his gut. "What do you know about making peace with anything and moving forward?"

She paled visibly and a bitter smile turned her lips. "More than you can possibly imagine. But this isn't about me, it's about you. You can't do everything you used to be able to do. You can't rush out onto the battlefield and maim and kill anymore. Boy, I can understand why you'd miss *that*," she said in scathing tones. "But there are a lot of other things you could be doing. Much more productive things than sitting around in the dark, crying in your beer and having one pity party after another."

She just wouldn't get it. "And what would you suggest, Ms. Rose? Hire myself to the local carny for their freak show?"

She threw her hands up in exasperation. "If that strokes your sore ego, have at it. But you might try something a little more productive. Open another group home. *Open ten.* Lord knows there are plenty of needy kids to fill them, and you're sitting on a pile of money you don't know what to do with."

Frustration pounded through his veins. "If opening another group home was an option I would have done it. But it's not. The one I have now is exceptional because of the people I have running it. And finding those people wasn't easy. I must have gone through fifteen employees before I found the right ones. And I found out who was good and who was bad by dropping in during every odd hour of the night and day. By talking extensively with the children. But I can't do that anymore. I scare the kids to death."

She hesitated, and he could see her reevaluating the argument. She drew a deep breath and let it out slowly.

"Have you given the kids a chance to get used to the new you?"

He laughed bitterly, sadly. "Yeah, the new me, that's rich. Have you forgotten, Ms. Rose, that you almost jumped out of your skin when you first saw me?"

A pink tinge colored her cheeks. "I remember. And I'm not telling you that the scar isn't startling. It is at first. But once the surprise wears off, it's just a scar." A hint of a smile turned her lips. "Actually, when you lift that brow just so, it's a downright sexy scar."

He shook his head in disgust. "Do you feel so sorry for me you think you have to lie to me?"

She grimaced at his rebuke, but her gaze locked onto his with startling intensity. "What I think is that you're a good man, Jason Kent, in a world that needs good men. And I think you should stop hiding up here in your little castle while important battles are being lost in the real world." She turned away from him and strode to the door.

Hesitating at the open portal she turned back to him with a sad, vulnerable smile. "And quit worrying about the face. It's incredibly sexy. And you can trust me on that one, because if I hadn't given up men I'd be knocking at your door." Without another word, she slipped out of the office, pulling the door closed behind her.

His heart stopped and then started again with the sharp force of a mule's kick. Did he hear what he just thought he'd heard? Did she say his face was incredibly sexy? That she'd be knocking at his door if she hadn't given up on men?

He shook his head. Even if she had said those things she couldn't have meant them. She was just trying to make him feel better.

But what if she did mean them?

The little voice, uninvited and unwelcome, sounded

from a place deep inside him. A place uncomfortably close to his heart. He shook his head. Great, now he was talking to himself. But he couldn't keep from silently answering the insistent voice. I'm sure she didn't mean them. She even qualified the last statement, remember? "If I hadn't given up men." She made sure I wouldn't expect her to step up to the plate and prove her claim.

But she looked like she meant it. She even looked a little sad, as if she might miss having a man in her life.

Maybe she is sad. Maybe she does miss having a man in her life. That doesn't mean she wants anything to do with me.

Maybe. Maybe not. One thing's for sure, you won't find out if she is interested unless you make some kind of move on her.

A cold sweat broke out on his palms. Oh no. I'm not setting myself up for that rejection.

It won't be the first time a woman's told you no.

No, but it would be the worst. She wouldn't be turning me down because she didn't like me. She'd be turning me down strictly because I have a bum leg and an ugly face.

That's a coward's excuse.

So what?

So ask the lady out, damn it.

A sardonic laugh echoed in his head. Ask her out where? We're stranded in the middle of a snowstorm, remember?

You'll think of something.

He stared at the door, hope and doubt pounding in his heart.

Ask her out.

Shut up. I'll think about it.

Chapter Six

All right, her nerves couldn't take the unknown a second longer. If Jason was going to strangle her for sticking her nose in his business she might as well get it over with. Because if he didn't kill her, starvation would.

She'd skipped breakfast in favor of getting the shutters opened before Jason wandered down for the morning, and she'd skipped lunch because she hadn't been brave enough to face Jason over chicken leftovers. If she skipped dinner, too, she wouldn't have to worry about Jason strangling her, she'd be dead by morning.

Which, when she thought about it, might not be so bad. She was making a mess of things here. It had been one thing for her to open the giant shutters—she'd thought she was doing Jason a favor. But telling him how to run his life was definitely stepping over the bounds. And then to tell him how sexy she thought he was… Lord, she was losing her mind. And her objectivity. Both personally and professionally.

She stared at the notebook and pen lying guiltily in the thick folds of the comforter next to her. After the fiasco in Jason's office this morning she'd headed back outside for a long walk through Montana's winter wonderland. But when her tennie-clad feet had gotten so cold she couldn't stand it any longer she'd come up here to the pink palace to crawl under the comforter and warm up.

Once she'd warmed up she'd tried to work on her story. But she was having serious second thoughts about writing the Jason Kent story. When she'd headed up this side of the mountain her objective had been clear. Get a story on Jason so she wouldn't have to face the sad little darlings at the group home. But now she wasn't sure she could sacrifice Jason Kent's privacy just because she couldn't face the children.

She'd known from the beginning that he had issues with his scar and limp. It had been evident from the moment he'd invited her into his house, but she hadn't realized until this morning how much pain her article would cause him.

And an article in a national magazine, an article that would have to mention his infirmities, would hurt him horribly. She couldn't do that. And where did that leave her? Out of a job, probably, if she showed up back at the magazine empty-handed. But right now, with her stomach growling for sustenance, that threat seemed far away, whereas facing Jason again…

She drew a deep breath and launched herself from the warm bed. If he was going to strangle her for being so pushy this morning she might as well get it over with. She slipped her tennies on and zipped down the stairs. Checking her watch, she strode down the hall to the kitchen. Six-thirty. Jason might still be in the kitchen eating dinner. Her stomach did a nervous rumba.

But when she pushed through the kitchen doors she found the bright room empty, the counters clear of dirty dishes and the usual mess associated with cooking. In fact, the only clue that Jason had been here at all was a single plate sitting in the middle of the counter, holding a sandwich and wrapped in plastic wrap. Angie strode over to the counter. On top of the plastic a small yellow Post-It had her name scrawled boldly across it.

A little smile tugged at her lips. Maybe he wasn't as angry as she'd thought. The tension in her chest eased just a little as she unwrapped the sandwich and lifted a corner of the bread. Tuna fish. Nothing fancy, but right now it sounded as good as steak. She grabbed a can of soda from the fridge, snatched up the plate and headed out of the kitchen in search of Jason.

She owed the man an apology, and if he was big enough to leave her a sandwich after she'd stomped all over his pride this morning, the least she could do was deliver it.

Taking a giant bite out of the sandwich, she backtracked down the hall to the foyer and across to the study. She nudged the sliding doors apart with an elbow and then slid one of them all the way open with her hip.

At the sound Jason glanced over from where he sat on the sofa, his cane resting next to him, his long, strong fingers curving around a giant brandy glass. He'd obviously been watching the fire, but now his attention was on her, his gaze dropping to the plate in her hand. "Good, you found the sandwich I left for you."

"I did, thank you. I was wondering, though, does this mean you're contemplating forgiving me for overstepping my bounds as a guest this morning *and* sticking my nose

where it didn't belong? Or just that you think I should
have a last meal before you strangle me?''

A hint of a smile pulled at his lips. ''Actually, it means
since I didn't see you wander down to the kitchen all day,
I thought you might be hungry.''

She chuckled softly, leaning against the door frame.
''Starving. Thank you.'' She took a bite of the sandwich,
chewing with relish as her stomach anxiously awaited the
nourishing fare.

He did indeed seem to have forgiven her. And she
briefly considered not going out of her way to remind him
about this morning by offering her apology. But her conscience wouldn't let her off the hook quite so easily.

She chased the bite of tuna down with a giant swallow
of soda, drew a deep, fortifying breath and started talking
before she chickened out. ''I'm sorry about this morning.
I should have asked before I opened the shutters. And I
certainly had no business telling you how to live your
life.''

''Let's call it even shall we? You might have stuck your
nose in some places where it didn't belong, but I had no
business yelling at you for opening the shutters, either.''

His lips straightened into a hard line and he flicked his
wrist, sending the amber liquor in the large bowl-like
glass spinning. ''I wasn't really angry with you for opening them. I was angry that by doing so you reminded me
that I couldn't. Which is certainly not your problem. It's
mine. And I had no business taking my anger out on
you.''

Relief poured through her. He was letting her off the
hook. She realized she'd been holding her breath, and now
she let it out in a rush. ''God, I'm glad that's over with.''

He chuckled wryly. ''Me, too. Would you like a snifter
of cognac? This is a very good brand.''

She raised a brow. "How good?"

A small smile pulled at his lips. "The best."

She waved away the offer. "No thanks. Somehow the idea of mixing 'the best' cognac with a tuna sandwich seems a bit incongruous, doesn't it?"

"You might be right about that," he conceded, his lips twitching upward again.

"I might be right about a lot of things." She gave him a teasing grin. "You should give it some thought."

He raised a warning brow. "I wouldn't press my luck if I were you. I hadn't meant that sandwich as your last meal but that doesn't mean it can't be."

She laughed, taking another bite of sandwich and strolling over to the sofa. "Care if I join you?"

He waved his free hand over the sofa. "I'd love the company."

She toed off her tennies and dropped into the corner opposite him. Swinging her legs onto the cushions, she stretched them out before her. Her toes were so close to Jason's thigh, his heat radiated against the soles of her feet. She wiggled her toes, enjoying the tactile pleasure. His heat was cozy. Comforting.

Jason's gaze dropped to the tiny space between her feet and his thigh.

She wiggled her toes again, smiling. "Do they stink?"

He looked up, tiny flags of guilt coloring his cheeks.

Oh dear, she'd washed her socks last night so they shouldn't, but maybe they did. Embarrassment heating her own cheeks, she started to pull her feet away.

"No." He reached out and grabbed one of her ankles. "They're fine. Leave them." His rough voice was even rougher than normal, but it didn't seem to be anger that had put the strain there.

She gave him a questioning look.

He shook his head, smiling ruefully. "I was just think-ing about the first night I saw you. You'd changed into my robe and your feet were bare."

If that was supposed to give her a hint about what was going on, it failed. "And?" she prompted.

The corner of his mouth twitched. "Your toenails were painted."

Now she was beginning to get it. A little smile pulled at her lips. "You like painted toenails."

He shook his head and chuckled, the sound caught somewhere between bemusement and humor, as if he himself couldn't believe the fascination. "I think I've been locked up in this mausoleum too long without female company."

She laughed softly, stretching her feet back down and giving his thigh a gentle, teasing nudge. "Maybe. But if you have, it's your own fault."

He raised that warning brow again.

She shook her head and gave him another nudge, his tantalizing heat soaking into her toes. "Save it, Kent. I'm only giving you one chance to strangle me, and you al-ready passed it by."

She set her soda on the coffee table, settled her plate securely in her lap and took another bite of sandwich. "So what are you doing in here? Beyond sitting and watching the fire?"

He raised the glass in his hand. "Beyond sitting and watching the fire I'm enjoying a fine snifter of cognac. And…" He hesitated for a moment, but only for a mo-ment. "And trying to decide the best way to ask you out on a date."

Surprise surged through her. She froze, her sandwich halfway to her mouth. "A date?" she squeaked.

His expression turned wry. "Yes, a date. You know,

when a man takes a woman to dinner, or a movie, or somewhere nice where they can enjoy each other's company? Of course, I can't really take you out anywhere here because of the storm. But I could fix us a nice, romantic dinner here.''

A thousand emotions swirled to life inside her. Excitement, pleasure, all the feminine thrills any woman feels when a handsome, desirable man asks her out on a date. But mixing with those heart-thumping emotions was also despair. Because it didn't matter that a handsome, desirable man had asked her out. She couldn't accept.

She set her sandwich back on her plate, reality sweeping in like a black cloud. ''I know what a date is, Jason. It's just been a while since anyone's asked me out on one.'' She tried to keep her voice even, matter-of-fact, but she sounded as weary as she suddenly felt.

He gave her a dubious look. ''Hard to believe. You're a beautiful woman.''

She plowed her fingers through her hair. ''Yeah, well, I've sworn off men, remember? I'm very careful not to give out signals that invite inquiries.''

''You weren't so careful this morning.''

She dropped her gaze to the plate in her lap. She might have made a bigger mistake this morning than she'd thought. But still, she couldn't be sorry for it. The idea of Jason Kent sitting up here wasting his life because he thought he looked like a monster incensed her at the deepest level. She gave a frustrated sigh. ''No, I wasn't.''

''Did you say what you did just because you felt sorry for me?'' His words had a sudden, sharp edge.

She jerked her gaze up from her lap and met his head on. ''No. I said it because you were behaving like an idiot, and it was the truth. But it doesn't matter how much I'm attracted to you—''

"It matters to me," he broke in quietly.

Her heart squeezed in her chest. His naked honesty sent wave after wave of yearning through her. After her accident she'd known no man would choose a half woman over a whole one, so she'd put her dreams of marriage and family aside and pursued her career with a vengeance. But that didn't mean she could look at Jason and see his desire and not want it.

It just meant she couldn't have it. "I don't date, Jason. I just don't." She tried to sound emphatic, but the only thing she heard in her words was desperation.

She expected him to snap back with anger. Most men would if they thought they'd been led on and then shut down. But what she saw in his expression was quiet wondering. He cocked his head and watched her, his blue-eyed gaze intent. "Do I at least get to know why?"

Panic scrambled up her spine. She couldn't tell him. Even after five years the words were too painful to utter aloud. But even if she could tell him, she wouldn't. The desire in his eyes was like a balm to her aching spirit, and if she told him why she'd sworn off men, it would disappear. She couldn't face that right now, but he deserved some kind of answer. She'd been the one to open her big mouth this morning, leading him on. "Let's just say that being left at the altar once is enough for any woman."

Surprise lifted his brows. "What happened?"

She shook her head trying to shake loose the old memories, the old pains, the old sorrows. "Things just fell apart between Steven and me."

He gave her a wry smile. "Which means that even if we sit here until spring you're not going to tell me, are you?"

She returned the smile. "No."

He hesitated, as if he'd like to pursue the subject, but

then he let it go with a dismissive wave of his hand. "Fine, let's talk about what you'd like to do on our date."

She gave an exasperated sigh. "Jason, did you hear anything I said?"

"I've got news for you, Angie. Beyond the fact that some poor sap with no judgement and less heart left you standing at the altar, you said damned little. And I'm not proposing marriage, so you don't have to worry that I'll stand you up at the altar—something I would never do to a woman, by the way. If I got far enough along to ask her to marry me, I'd damned well know she was the one. There wouldn't be any last minute—"

"You're digressing, Jason."

He flashed an unapologetic smile. "You're right. Let's back up to, I'm not proposing marriage. Realistically, once those plows make it up the road, it's safe to assume our paths will never cross again. You'll go your way and I'll go mine. What could possibly be the harm in us spending one evening enjoying each other's company?"

Shock raced through her system. Shock and… excitement. Jason wasn't talking about a date that might lead to another date and eventually the discovery of her secret. He was just talking about a single evening.

She pulled her legs up tailor fashion and leaned forward, giving him her full attention. "I'm listening."

Triumph glittered in his eyes. "Good. I'm thinking tomorrow night, you, me, a bottle of good champagne and a table full of gourmet foods here in this room with a roaring fire and a little Rachmaninoff playing over the sound system. Quiet conversation and easy touching."

Feminine anticipation fizzed in her veins. But a hint of unease ran beside it. She raised her gaze to Jason's. "Easy touching?"

A knowing smile touched his lips. "Easy touching

means you get to decide when and where and how long it goes on.''

A shiver that should have had her blushing scarlet shimmied over her, settling in a most erotic spot, but she didn't blush and she didn't try to hide her excitement, either. She set her plate down, stood and paced eagerly around the room.

''Do I get a kiss at the end of the night?'' Her question was just a little more breathless than she intended, but she couldn't keep the hope and exhilaration from her words.

Jason's nostrils flared wide and his sapphire eyes darkened toward midnight. ''You get whatever you want.''

Jason watched Angie slip out of the study, his heart pounding with the force of a dozen concussion grenades going off one after the other, his blood rushing in his ears. She'd said yes. Well, she hadn't said yes specifically. But asking for a kiss qualified as a yes in his book.

He was pretty sure it also meant she didn't intend to go any further than a kiss. But he could settle for that.

Settle? Fifteen minutes ago when he'd been sitting here trying to find enough nerve to ask her to spend an evening with him, as a man not a host, he'd been willing to settle for dinner and a good-night-I-enjoyed-myself handshake afterward. But a kiss... Angie's soft, bee-stung lips against his. Her curvy little body pressed against him. Oh man, he'd sell his soul for that.

Chapter Seven

*T*he evening had arrived.

Angie ran her brush through her hair for the thousandth time, her nerves vibrating, her heart pounding.

A date.

The sharp ache of longing squeezed her heart as she stared at her flushed face and over-bright eyes in the mirror. She'd been thinking how nice it would be to sit across from Jason and see his interest and feel his touch and pretend that even if he knew everything about her, that look wouldn't change.

A pipe dream. But for this one night she could pretend. Because she wouldn't be around long enough for Jason to discover her secret. According to the noon newscast, the plows would have even the most remote roads cleared by tomorrow. She'd already called her rental car agency and they'd promised to send a car for her as soon as she let them know the plows were through. Tonight was all they were ever going to have. One night to enjoy a little conversation and a little ''easy touching'' and then she'd be gone. One night to create a lovely memory that she could tuck away for the lonely nights ahead.

Providing she found the nerve to leave this room. Lord, she was a nervous wreck. It had been so long since she'd done this. Tried to be pretty and entertaining and...

For pity's sake, she was acting like an idiot. She could do this. Enough stalling. She tossed her brush on the dressing table and gave herself one last look in the mirror.

Not that there was much to look at. Beyond washing her jeans and sweater, there hadn't been much she could do to spruce herself up. She'd hoped to find a loose necklace or a pair of earrings in her purse. She often wore jewelry to business meetings and then took it off afterward, tossing it in her purse until she remembered to take it out. But a thorough search of her giant bag had turned up nothing. Except...

She stared down at her toenails with a wicked smile. She had discovered a half-full bottle of party-time-red nail polish. Her toenails were now glistening red and ready to rock.

And the party was waiting for her downstairs.

Squaring her shoulders, she took a final, deep breath and strode toward the door. The naked hall floors were cold on her bare feet, so she rushed down the hall, down the stairs and across the foyer, coming to a halt in front of the big mahogany doors leading to the study.

She didn't let herself think, didn't let the panic bubbling up in her send her running back to the safety of her room. She took another quick, deep breath, slid the doors open and slipped inside.

At the sound, Jason turned toward her from where he

slowly paced in front of the fireplace, the golden eagle topping his cane glinting beneath his hand in the soft light.

And Lord, he was gorgeous.

He'd put on a pair of dark gray dress slacks that accented the length of his legs and the leanness of his hips. And the light blue dress shirt he'd donned showed off his broad shoulders and intensified the color of his eyes. Thankfully, he hadn't gone completely formal and added a tie. He'd left the collar and top button of his shirt undone, leaving a small triangle of tanned, male skin exposed and keeping the mood somewhat casual.

But that small concession didn't make her feel much better. She gave him a mock scowl. "You dressed, you rat."

His gaze slid over her as voraciously as hers had slid over him, finally coming to rest on her bare feet. His eyes sparkled to life and his lips curved in a sexy smile. "So did you."

A giant wave of feminine delight surged through her, thrilling her senses and kicking her self-confidence back into full swing. She wiggled her toes. "Yeah, I guess I did."

He looked up with that playful, sexy smile. "I *like* it."

She laughed softly, moving on into the room. "So do I." Excitement shimmered through her as she took in the effort he'd put into the room. Tall, white candles sat on every surface, their flickering flames bathing the room in soft light and dancing shadows. She turned back to him with a beaming smile. "Beautiful."

He dipped his head and leaned forward in a quarter bow, acknowledging the praise, and then he waved his hand toward the sofa. "Champagne?"

She turned, noticing for the first time the small table

laden with food and the bottle of champagne chilling in a stand next to it. "Definitely."

He walked to the little table and lifted the champagne from the bucket. She took the two champagne flutes from the shelf beneath the table and held them up. "Just in case it spews."

He gave her a confident smile. "Only amateurs spew the champagne." And his expression clearly said he wasn't an amateur—at opening a bottle of champagne or anything else he had planned for the night.

Heat slid through her veins, settling low in her belly as he grabbed the bottle in one hand and carefully worked the cork up with the other, those long, strong fingers in complete control. Lordy, if he didn't get that cork out soon, she was going to melt on the spot.

Finally the cork gave with a soft pop, and he poured the effervescent liquid into her glass. She took a giant swallow, trying to calm her nerves and cool the heat sizzling through her.

Jason raised his brows. "Should I have brought two bottles out?"

She laughed. "I'm sure one will do the trick." She leaned forward, perusing the scrumptious fare on the table, trying to ignore the goose bumps Jason's closeness was raising on her skin. A lovely wedge of Brie oozed at center court with a small square of pâté and an assortment of meats and other cheeses arranged around it. Crackers and thick slices of french bread were neatly arranged on the platter while olives and nuts and chocolates filled the small spaces between the delicacies.

She pointed to several slices of meat snuggled up to the pâté. "What's that?"

"Smoked duck."

"Ooooh, that sounds good." She lifted a small piece

to her mouth. The tender, smoky meat practically melted on her tongue. She licked her lips and closed her eyes, savoring the delicacy. ''That'll definitely do.''

When she opened her eyes she found Jason staring at her, his midnight gaze locked on her lips with a hungry-wolf expression that sent sharp tingles of awareness skittering over her skin.

''Oh, Jason. Don't start that now. We'll both be in trouble.'' She leaned down, retrieved the plates that had been stored with the champagne flutes and handed one to him. ''Let's eat.''

His hand closed around the white china, and he started filling his plate from the wide array of foods. ''Did—'' He had to stop and clear his throat. ''Did you get any work done today?''

Oh no, she was not going to ruin tonight wondering what she was going to do about her article. She gave him a nonchalant shrug and changed the subject. ''Some. Did you make a killing on the stock market?''

''Nope, dropped a bundle,'' he admitted with—if she wasn't mistaken—glee in his voice.

She lifted her gaze from the table. Yep, he was grinning from ear to ear. And then she remembered that yesterday he'd been complaining about his Midas touch. She shook her head in disbelief. ''Lucky you.''

She finished filling her plate and dropped into the closest corner of the leather couch. Just as she had the other day, she swung her legs onto the cushions. ''Come on, Jason, take those fancy loafers off. My feet are freezing, which means they need your feet to keep them warm.'' She threw him a teasing smile with just a hint of challenge in it.

He met her gaze head on, then slowly, deliberately toed off one shoe and then the other. Keeping his gaze locked on her, he dropped into the corner opposite her and swung his legs up, placing the soles of his feet squarely against hers.

Heat sizzled up her legs, sending a delicate shiver to her core. His feet dwarfed hers, and their tantalizing heat woke up the female in her with a bang. She wiggled her toes against his, reveling in the feel of male against female.

He gave a mock shiver and shot her an innocent look. "Your feet are frozen. Maybe you should scoot up, put them in my lap and I'll warm them with my hands."

She shook her head, a giddy little laugh bubbling up. "Oh no, I'm not falling for that. They're warming up just fine." Better than just fine, but she didn't think it would be wise to share that information with him yet.

She took another deep, cooling sip of champagne. "You want to tell me how you lost your bundle today?"

He shook his head. "It wasn't all that spectacular. Why don't I tell you a little about Kent House? Even without your notebook and pen, you're bound to remember the important parts. And, by the time they dig us out, you're not going to have much time at the home for interviews."

Her stomach clenched. Kent House was the last thing she wanted to talk about. Tonight was about fantasy and could-have-beens. She didn't want to think about could-never-bes. Not with the candlelight burning and the champagne bubbling in her veins and Jason sending erotic little jolts through her feet.

But if she completely closed him down on the subject again, he might get suspicious, and she didn't want that, either. She needed a bit of reporter's sleight of hand. "Let's start with why you decided to build Kent House." She popped another bite of smoked duck into her mouth,

hoping Jason wouldn't notice that the subject had shifted
from the group home to him.

"I didn't really plan it. It just happened." He took a
sip of champagne and then set his glass on the floor next
to the sofa.

Yeah, right. She gave his foot a little push. "Jason, an
orphanage doesn't just spring up and become one of the
most acclaimed homes for difficult-to-adopt children by
accident."

"No, that part took a lot of hard work. But the idea
itself *was* an accident." He gave his lips a wry twist. "Or,
as my boss so succinctly put it, a moronic, half-assed,
bleeding heart act of stupidity."

Her brows shot up. "I *do* get to hear that story, don't
I?"

"Not if I can help it. Tyner was right. We got lucky
and things worked out in the end, and eventually Kent
House came out of it. But it could have been a major
disaster, for everyone concerned. Besides—" his sapphire
gaze took on a sensual glint "—I'd rather tell you how
beautiful you are in the candlelight. How much I like the
feel of your skin against mine. How much I'd like to be
touching a whole lot more than your feet."

Heat raced through her like the sun dawning on a dark,
dark day, but she didn't let herself be diverted. Not yet.
It was much too early in the evening for that. She wanted
to savor this night, not rush into it. "Don't change the
subject. I want to hear about Kent House's conception."

He grimaced but dutifully launched into the story.
"First you have to understand that as a merc I spent a lot
of time in third world countries, countries inundated by
war and poverty...and lost, hungry children."

He shook his head, the memory still obviously bothering him. "They scrounged in the garbage to eat, drank

their water out of the gutters and laid down alone in a dark corner at night to sleep. And there wasn't a damned thing I could do about it but toss them my rations and hope they made it through one more night.'' He ran a hand down his face, his feet moving restlessly against hers.

She pressed back, offering what comfort she could. But she didn't say anything. She just waited quietly for him to go on.

A sip of champagne, a bite of cracker later, he did. ''Then, about six years ago, Tyner sent eight of us to a little village just east of hell's half acre to help support the government troops against some local guerillas. The first day I was there I ran into this little girl.''

A smile turned his lips. ''Maria. She was a cutie with these big, brown eyes. Beautiful eyes. But they were so sad. And she was way too thin. I tossed her a can of rations.'' His smile got a little wider. ''Those gorgeous eyes doubled in size and she scampered away with her prize. And I figured that would be the last I saw of her, but the next day she showed back up. With a rock.''

She cocked her head in question. ''A rock?''

He laughed softly. ''A rock. It was a pretty rock, really. And Maria obviously thought it had value.''

Her heart clenched as she realized the child's intent. ''Oh God, she was trading you for your rations.''

''She couldn't have been more than four then, but she'd figured out that survival tactic overnight.'' He shook his head as if he still couldn't believe the child's ingenuity, nor her desperation. ''Anyway, I made the trade, and every day for the next week she showed up with whatever she'd managed to scrounge for the next swap. And all during that time I asked around about her, trying to find out if she had a family or anyone looking after her.''

"But she didn't."

He shook his head. "No."

"And?" she prompted, rubbing her feet against his, needing the contact now as much as he.

His lips hardened into a thin straight line. "And then it was time for our team to go. The plane was waiting for us, its engines screaming in the hot noon sun—and there she was, with those pretty brown eyes and a broken piece of green glass clutched in her hand. Her bartering chip for the day. And I couldn't stand the thought of leaving her."

Her fingers tightened on her own glass. She could imagine his anger and frustration as he stood in the plane headed for a land of peace and plenty while the tiny, defenseless girl remained behind in a land of war and poverty. Her heart ached at the helplessness he must have felt. "Is that why you built Kent House—because you had to leave Maria behind?" The thought of the little girl being left in a village where guerillas and government soldiers were fighting an uncertain battle was just too sad to contemplate.

A wry smile slowly appeared on his lips. "Not exactly. You see, the plane that was about to take us home was private. Very private. We didn't file flight plans. We didn't go through customs. We just slipped quietly in and out of the country, carte blanche, thanks to Uncle Sam. And I thought, what the hell? Nobody's going to miss her here. So I just scooped her up and took her into the plane with me."

Relief for little Maria, amazement at Jason's action and apprehension for the problems his rash act could have caused swirled inside her. "And *then* what happened? You do know you could have ended up in jail, don't you? And not necessarily a clean, relatively safe American jail. You could just as easily have ended up in a rat-infested, let's-torture-our-prisoners-today kind of jail in whatever country you'd airlifted poor Maria out of. *And the political fallout.* Lord Jason, you could have caused an international incident."

His expression turned rueful. "Funny, I think that's what my boss thought when the pilot radioed ahead to let him know we had a little stowaway on board, because when I stepped off the plane twelve hours later at our private airstrip in North Dakota, Tyner was standing there ready to kick my ass. Just the idea of the political fallout Maria could have caused had him ready to slit my throat. Until I brought Maria out of the plane."

He chuckled softly. "The second Tyner saw her, he was a goner. Those big brown eyes of hers just sucked him in. And then, *then* he suddenly remembers, oh yeah, he has this friend who's married to this wonderful woman and they've been trying to adopt a little girl from China for two years with no success, and hey, wouldn't Maria be just perfect for them?" He laughed harder now as if remembering a great joke.

"And is that where Maria is now? With Tyner's friends?" She couldn't keep the hope from her voice.

He nodded. "She's doing great. She's in the fourth grade, still pretty as a picture. And those eyes. They'll stop your heart."

Tears rushed to her eyes and a sappy smile turned her lips. "Good job, soldier. Now tell me how you pulled it off. Tyner might have been as enamored of the little girl as you, but something tells me the hard-core politicians worried about their next election and the tough officers at Immigration might not have been so easily persuaded."

He gave a disparaging huff. "No, they weren't. They were a royal pain in the—"

She gave his foot a sharp nudge. "Ah-ah-ah. Be nice."

"Why? They weren't nice. At least the Immigration guys weren't."

She took a sip of champagne. "How did you pull it off then?"

A sly smile replaced his scowl. "Your hard-core politicians. Remember the other day when you asked what kind of merc I was, and I told you God and country?"

She nodded.

"Well, Tyner's company only does government work. When Uncle Sam's drones have nasty little situations where they need results fast and can't risk any link to the U.S., Tyner's the first man they call. As a result, Tyner and every man in his company have made political connections. Most of us have more than one senator or congressman or major businessman who thinks he owes us a favor or two. Tyner and I weren't shy about pulling ours in for Maria."

Wonder washed through her. Wonder and awe and admiration. "And so you saved a little girl."

He shrugged his shoulders. "I don't know that I saved her. I gave her a better life." No bravado, no bragging, no pat on the back, just a quiet statement of fact.

Amazement slid through her. The man didn't have a clue about the enormity of what he had done, the miracle of what he had accomplished. She gave his foot another nudge. "So tell me how Kent House came out of all this?"

He made a face. "Oh, it became this big joke with the guys, you know? Kent's orphanage. And one day it just clicked. I had all the money I'd been earning in the stock market and nothing to do with it. Back then I was planning to marry eventually, but Ms. Right hadn't wandered along yet, and I had more money than I needed to play house with anyway, so I figured, why not? I knew first-hand how dismal the system for orphans in the U.S. could be, and I thought a good home, run by great people would be a good idea."

A good idea. Another simple statement, claiming neither recognition nor accolades for himself. But there had been nothing simple about what he'd done, in either the rescue of Maria or the building of Kent House. Both acts had taken fortitude and courage and boundless generosity.

Her heart turned over in her chest. Jason Kent was the kind of man young girls dreamed of. Men like Sir Galahad and Robin Hood and the Knights of The Round Table. He was the type of man she, too, had once dreamed of. The type of man she could no longer have.

Except for tonight.

A tremulous smile pulled at her lips. She caught his sapphire gaze and gave his foot a gentle nudge. "Kiss me."

Sapphire darkened to midnight blue and before she had time to draw in her next breath he'd set his plate down, set hers next to it, pushed himself to his feet and pulled her up into a light embrace.

She stood mere inches from him, his hands resting on her shoulders, his heat soaking into her, his breath stirring the hair on her forehead.

"We could do this sitting down, but I want to feel you against me. All of you." He stretched one hand, rubbing his thumb ever so gently over her collarbone. "From this delicate bone right down to your sexy little toes."

Jason's desire sent her blood crashing through her veins. "I like this, standing next to you. Feeling your heat, your strength." She stepped closer, overlapping his toes with hers, resting her hands at his waist, letting their clothes brush softly over each other.

A low growl sounded in his throat and he bumped his

hips against hers, seemingly more from reflex than intent, his hard maleness seeking her softer femininity. Then he leaned his head down, grazing her ear with his lips. "How do you like your kisses? Soft and sweet? Slow and easy? Or hot and deep?"

Her knees went weak and she had to tighten her grip at his waist to keep her balance. A soft, helpless laugh fell from her lips. "Lord, I've forgotten. They all sound good." Another giddy laugh. "Too good."

A low, smoky laugh joined hers. "Let's start at the top then." He tipped her chin up, his fingers warm and gentle against her skin, his midnight gaze hot and intent.

She closed her eyes just as his lips settled, as light as a butterfly's kiss, on her cheek. Her cheek, her eyelid, her nose and finally...finally her lips. Warm and soft and oh, oh so sweet.

Trying to get more of him she ran her hands up his sides, reveling in the feel of hard muscle, the feel of his heat soaking through his shirt, the feel of his breathing, short and hard. She arched against him, wanting more, needing more than the light, sweet little kisses. She raised herself on her toes, reaching for more.

But just as she tried to deepen the kiss, Jason lifted his head. "Ready for step two?" His normally rough voice was made even rougher by desire.

Her mind went blank and her hands tightened at his waist, trying to pull him closer. "Step two?"

He tried to smile, but he was drawn as tightly as she was and the gesture turned into a tense twist of his lips. "Slow and easy."

She couldn't keep the frustrated little growl from sounding in her throat. "I don't suppose we could jump straight to hot and deep, could we?"

Midnight blue flashed to black and then his lips crashed
down on hers. Hot and hard and urgent.

She surged against him, opening her mouth for him,
letting him inside, taking him inside. Meeting him thrust
for thrust.

His hands dropped to her hips and as his mouth ravaged
hers he pulled her against him.

And God, it felt good. Feeling Jason's passion, his heat.
His body wrapped around hers. His hardness pressing
against her femininity. He wanted her.

And she wanted him. She moved against him, her fingers digging into his skin, a sharp feminine tingle explod-
ing along her nerves.

He pulled her closer, sending his tongue deeper into her
mouth, dragging her hips once again over his hard length.

She groaned as another sharp wave of pleasure crashed
over her. Groaned and moved into the kiss, into the
rhythm his hands were setting at her hips. Reveling in the
proof of his desire. Reveling in the sharp ache of need
building like a hot fire inside her.

He dragged his mouth from hers, his breathing hard and
heavy. "Should we take this somewhere else?"

Yes.

No. Her hands clenched the material of his shirt. "Oh
God, we have to stop."

"Why?" He ran one of his hands up her ribs, his touch
quick, urgent. "I won't disappoint you, Angie. I know I
seem beat up, but the grenade that took out my knee left
everything else intact. I can take care of you."

She shook her head again, frustration and pain settling
in her heart. Pain and frustration and an emptiness that
threatened to swallow her whole. "I can't, Jason. Not because I think you'll disappoint me. But because I'll disappoint you. I'm not what you need."

His hands tightened at her hips. "Stop telling me what I need, damn it. I'll take whatever you can give and consider myself the luckiest man on earth."

She shook her head desperately. "No, you won't. You'll want more. You *deserve* more. And when you realize I can't give you more, you'll leave me behind. And I can't take that again, Jason. I just can't." She pulled herself from his embrace and fled from the room.

"Angie, wait!"

But she didn't stop her headlong flight. She flew across the foyer, up the stairs and into the darkness of the hall above.

Jason watched her go, his hands clenched into fists, his groin pounding in a steady, painful ache. What the *hell* had just happened?

Frustration and anger poured through him. Had she run away because the idea of going to bed with a cripple had repulsed her? His gut clenched. It was certainly a possibility. Kissing a man was one thing, going to bed with him quite another.

But she hadn't seemed put off or disgusted when she'd said no. She'd seemed...afraid of something. And what the hell was this nonsense about her not being able to give him what he needed? Just *what* did she think he needed?

Chapter Eight

Angie stood in her room, staring across the sea of pink and out the giant, mullioned window. The wind was howling like a deranged wolf this morning, sending white snowflakes into the air in a manic dance of sparkling crystals. A perfect metaphor for her current mood. Restless and just a little bit frantic.

Last night's kiss had rocked her right down to her lonely little soul.

It had been....wonderful. But hot on the heels of that wonder came embarrassment and fear.

Lord, she'd run out of the room like a crazy person. And she never, *never* should have spouted her worst fears to Jason. The fear that he would find her wanting. She didn't want him to start wondering whether there was something wrong with her.

The look of desire she'd seen in his eyes last night had been too nice. Too special. She didn't want it replaced with the same look of pity and disappointment she'd seen in Steven's eyes after he'd found out just how much she'd lost when that drunk driver had come around the corner on her side of the road.

But she'd had to say something. She couldn't let Jason think she'd ended the kiss because she didn't want him. When nothing, absolutely nothing, was further from the truth.

She gave her head a frustrated shake. Lord, she'd made a mess of everything. She looked down at the notebook crunched in her hand. The notes she'd taken on Jason Kent. The notes she would never be able to use.

With a frustrated sigh she tossed the notebook on the dresser and stalked over to the giant window. Now what? She had no story, which meant she'd probably be without a job once she got home. And this morning...she had to face Jason Kent again.

Lord, what must he think of her after the way she'd dashed out of the study last night? She pulled her gaze from the swirling snow and rubbed her eyes. The only saving grace was that Jason wouldn't have much time to ask questions. And she wouldn't have to turn on the spit of embarrassment for long because she'd run out of the room like some histrionic heroine in an old movie. As soon as the plows made it up the road, she'd call the rental agency and a car would be on its way to pick her up.

Her heart clenched. Even though she felt relieved that Jason wouldn't have time to discover her secret, the thought of leaving left an empty place in her chest. She was going to miss him—a lot. And those kisses—that soft, sweet kiss and that hot, deep, I've-got-to-have-you-now kiss—were going to be damned hard to walk away from.

But leaving was the only solution. She didn't have anything but friendship to offer any man, and she didn't think

Jason was interested in being just friends. So today would have to be goodbye, and now was as good a time as any to thank Jason for his hospitality and say that goodbye.

She drew a deep fortifying breath, strode from the pink palace into the dark stone hall and hurried down the staircase to the cavernous foyer below.

Across the entrance hall one of the sliding doors to the study stood open, the distinct sounds of a television drifting from the room. She glanced at her watch. Noon. Jason must be watching the news. The easiest way to keep track of the state's road cleanup.

She strode across the foyer, her footsteps echoing hollowly against the massive stone walls. At the study she leaned into the room, not quite brave enough to enter. Jason sat across the room on the sofa, his attention fixed on the television. "Hi," she said.

At the sound of her voice he glanced her way, muted the sound from the TV and shifted on the sofa to face her, his sapphire gaze steady, direct. "Hi." He sat, quietly, watching her, waiting perhaps to see what she would say.

She could feel the flush climbing up her neck and over her cheeks. She might as well get it over with. He deserved to hear it. "Sorry about last night."

He shrugged, his gaze never leaving hers. "I'm not. I enjoyed every minute of it." A quick, wry smile turned his lips. "Right up until the minute you ran away."

For the thousandth time in the last twelve hours she wished she'd handled the situation better. But she couldn't undo it now. "I'm sorry. Things got out of control and I just panicked." She ran a distraught hand through her hair.

He cocked his head to the side. "You want to talk about it?"

"*God no*—I mean—" Heat scalded her cheeks. She sighed in frustration, then took a deep breath. "I mean, I acted like an idiot and I'd rather not rehash it. But I would like to thank you for the evening. It was really quite wonderful."

He stared at her long and thoughtfully. Finally he seemed to come to some decision. "I have to ask, Angie. How will you disappoint me?"

Her heart stopped and then slammed against her ribs in a fast, erratic rhythm. The question she dreaded most. She searched frantically for a diversion, but her mind only sputtered in alarm.

When she didn't answer, Jason went on. "Last night you said we had to stop because you would disappoint me. I was just wondering why you thought that."

Panic pounded in her ears. Thank God she was leaving today or this would be the start of it. The questions, the doubts, and if he ever found out her reason, the inevitable decision that she wasn't quite what he thought. Or what he wanted.

Her palms broke out in a cold sweat, but she drew in a deep breath and tried to make herself sound convincing as she fobbed off the question. "Jason, it's not important. I told you I overreacted. Let's leave it at that, shall we?"

A smile with a bit of an edge curved his lips. "Oh, I see. My problems are fair game, but your problems are off-limits. Is that it?"

Guilt slid through her. It might seem that way to him, but there was a difference. His problems wouldn't stop him from being what he'd been before his accident, a good man with the strength and power and vision to make the world a better place. Nor would his injuries stop him from having what he'd *wanted* before the accident, a wife and children of his own. Once he got that into his head, his life would move on in the direction he'd always dreamed of.

Her problem fell into a whole different category. One she wasn't willing to discuss with him. "Listen, I'm sorry about running out on you last night. But there's no point in discussing it. I'm leaving today, remember? As soon as the plows dig us out. So I just came down to say good-bye and thank you for keeping me for the last week."

That edgy smile got a little bit wider. "I think there's plenty of point in discussing it. And if time is your only concern, fear not. As of this morning you have plenty of it."

Alarm ran up her spine. "What's that supposed to mean?"

He turned away from her and once again pointed the remote at the television. The sound slowly came up until the newscaster's voice was clear. "To recap today's leading story: all major highways have been closed in northern Montana. The surprise storm closing in on the area is expected to bring another foot of snow over the next three days and winds in excess of sixty miles an hour. Due to the previous heavy snowfall it is anticipated that the strong winds will close most roads with drifting snow within the next few hours. Residents are being asked to go home and stay there. With the exception of a few roads surrounding hospitals and police stations, plowing has been suspended until the storm has passed."

Panic slammed through her as Jason once again lowered the volume on the set. Three more days. Three more days before the storm was over. And then how much longer until the plows made it up this mountain?

She stared at the man across from her.

He stared back with the confidence of a panther who'd

spotted his prey and now simply sat quietly in the bushes knowing his chance to pounce would come.

She grabbed hold of the fear threatening to drown her and raised her chin. Now was not the time to show any weakness. "Three days or three years, Jason. I'm *not* going to talk about it."

He cocked a challenging brow. "Did you enjoy the kiss?"

Another sharp stab of panic told her she should lie, tell him she hadn't enjoyed it. But her conscience wouldn't let her say it. "Yes. But that doesn't mean—"

"It means we're going to talk about it. But not right now. I can see the panic in your eyes. We'll talk later when you've had time to calm down. And right now I need you to go close the shutters. The winds aren't bad yet, but they're going to get there fast. I don't want you climbing the walls when the winds are really howling."

"Oh Lord, the stained glass windows. I'll get them now." Grasping at the excuse to get away, she practically ran from the doorway.

It was a cowardly exit, but right now she was going to take any advantage she could get.

Ducking her head against the driving snow and ice, Angie carefully climbed up the slippery metal rungs set into the gray stone. Could things possibly get any worse? This storm was already whipping itself into a frenzy, the temperatures dropping by the minute and the winds getting stronger and stronger. And inside the house things were just as scary.

Jason wanted answers.

Answers she couldn't give him. Wouldn't give him.

Another sharp gust of wind hit her broadside, stinging her cheeks with icy little missiles. She was only halfway to the top; she had another ten feet to go before she could start closing shutters. Her foot slipped on the next rung and she had to scramble to regain her footing.

Lord, if she didn't start paying attention she was going to find herself in big trouble. But she couldn't concentrate on the task at hand. She was too busy trying to figure out how she was going to deal with Jason for the next however many days.

Her body tingled to life, her lips throbbing, hot and achy, as last night's kiss played over in her mind. Oh yeah, the perfect response if she wanted to *really* be in trouble. Ruthlessly stomping on those wayward feelings, she resolutely finished the climb to the top of the windows.

Carefully she began the process of sliding the massive wooden shutters closed and latching them tightly against the elements. A tinge of regret skittered through her as the luminous colors disappeared behind gray wood. But there wasn't anything for it. The artwork had to be protected.

She made her way slowly from window to window, pushing shutters shut and latching them tight. By the time she hit the last one her hands were frozen. With clumsy fingers she slid the last lock home.

Suddenly, over the low moan of the wind, she heard a piercing cry. She spun around on the metal rung, letting go with one hand so she could swivel her torso to look behind her toward the forest. A flash of red and blue and yellow was streaking down the hill. What on earth? She squinted against the blowing snow.

"Help, I can't stop!" the cry came again, high pitched and panicked.

Oh Lord, it was a child on a sled, an out-of-control sled

that was racing down the mountainside, headed straight for a collision with a giant pine.

"Roll off!" Angie shouted, scrambling the rest of the way down the ladder and jumping the last five feet to the ground. Regaining her balance, she started running for the forest. "Roll off the sled!"

But the little child didn't. He or she just gripped the rope tighter and screamed. And then everything happened at once. The sled's wide runners seemed to lose their grip on the snow, and the sled went spinning end over end down the mountain. The child was flung free, arms and legs and scarf tails flying this way and that as the little body flipped down the mountainside in a tiny ball of blue and yellow.

Angie ran harder, her heart trying to pound its way out of her chest.

The sled crashed into a tree, stopping its headlong flight. But, thankfully, the child simply lost momentum and came to a snowy halt as Angie closed the distance between them. She'd almost reached the child's side when a high, jubilant giggle erupted from the colorful pile of primary colors.

Oh God, he, she, it was okay. At least it was alive. Angie raced the last few steps and dropped to her knees next to the snow-coated bundle. "Are you okay?" Her voice was squeaky and breathless.

The child pushed onto its hands and knees, laughter still tumbling in the air, little yellow mittens digging into the snow. "I'm fine."

Relief poured through Angie at the child's reassurance—the little *girl's* reassurance. That was definitely the voice of a little girl.

Angie grabbed her shoulders, helping her to her feet.

"You scared me to death. What were you doing sledding down a hill covered with trees?"

The little girl brushed the snow from her chubby, red cheeks, her brows snapping together like tiny raven wings over her green eyes. "I didn't know how else to get down."

A smile pulled at Angie's lips. Cute kid. Spunky. Angie brushed a bunch of snow off the small shoulders, noticing that there didn't seem to be any kind of pain or disorientation in those bright green eyes. "Are you sure you're all right?"

The pint-sized girl started brushing the snow from her coat and pants, too. "Yeah. Who are you? Are you a friend of Jason's?"

"I'm Angie. I'm a guest of Jason's. Who are you?"

"I'm Jason's neighbor."

Neighbor? She hadn't seen any houses on her trip up Jason's road. She looked around the forest, trying to spot a house off in the distance that she'd overlooked before. "Where's your house? And who's out here with you?"

The little girl swept her mittened hand in a wide arc that encompassed the whole mountain. "My house is over there, and I'm by myself. Jason said I could come over anytime I want. So I came over to visit."

"By yourself? In this storm?" Angie couldn't keep the alarm from her voice. "Does your mother know where you are?"

The little munchkin gave her a cheeky grin. "She was busy when I left, so I just left a note."

A note, huh? Spunky...and a handful. Angie would bet her right hand this little one wasn't old enough to write yet. A shiver ran up her spine. Lord, if she hadn't been outside closing the shutters, if the sled had slammed into that tree, who knows how long it would have been before the mother figured out where to look for her child. In these weather conditions, she might never have found her.

Scenes of disaster flashing in her head, Angie gave the young girl a stern look. "You shouldn't wander away from home without telling someone. Particularly when the weather is this fierce. Your mother is probably scared to death. Come on, let's go give her a call right now. Before she calls out the National Guard," Angie added wryly.

"The National Guard?" The little girls eyes lit up with excitement. "Are those soldiers like Jason used to be?"

"Kind of. And I wouldn't look so thrilled if I were you. If your mother *has* called out the guard, you're probably going to be spending the next month in your room."

A quick grimace flashed across the girl's face. Obviously she hadn't thought of the repercussions of her little jaunt until now. But her smile quickly bounced back. "Don't worry. If she's mad, Jason can talk her out of it." She gave Angie a very adult look. "He's very persuasive, you know."

Angie raised a brow. "Persuasive, huh?"

The youngster nodded her head solemnly.

"Is that your new word for the day?"

The girl giggled the high, carefree sound only a child can produce. "Yesterday's word."

Uh-huh. "You never told me your name."

"Hallie." A proud smile suddenly turned the small, bow-shaped lips. "My mom picked that name."

Angie grasped Hallie's mittened hand. "Well, your mom has good taste, but we need to get inside before we freeze to death. Let's go."

She helped the little girl down the hillside, lifting her through the bigger snowdrifts and holding tight to the small hand while Hallie plowed her way through the others. When they finally reached the house Angie pulled her through the massive front door into the mansion's comforting warmth.

"Jason!" Angie hollered as she pulled off her coat, draped it over the coat rack and then went to work on Hallie's snow-encrusted gear.

Just as she pulled the little girl's mittens free she heard Jason's cane on the foyer's stone floor. She looked over her shoulder at him as she continued to work Hallie's frozen zipper free. "You have a little guest."

His brows shot toward his hairline. "Hallie? What are you doing here?"

"You said I could visit, remember?"

He headed toward them, his cane tapping, his brows pulled low over his eyes. "Yes, I remember. But how did you get here? Did Ms. Carmichael bring you?"

For the first time the little girl's expression became a little sheepish. She shook her stocking-capped head, snow flying loose. "No. I brought myself."

Jason stopped in his tracks, his complexion paling a shade. "You brought yourself? How?" His first question had been uttered in disbelief, but that last one had been spat like a general demanding an answer from one of his subordinates. An answer he knew he wasn't going to like.

No, he definitely wasn't going to like it, Angie thought, squelching the smile that tugged at her lips as she pulled Hallie's coat free. She had a feeling the little cherub was about to discover that one's actions had definite and sometimes unpleasant consequences. Hanging the small, bright blue coat on the coat rack with hers, Angie stepped out of the way so Jason and Hallie could talk without interference.

Hallie, too, seemed to understand that the hammer was about to fall. Her expression became downright meek. "I pulled my sled to the top of the hill and rode down."

Jason's complexion paled a little more, but his lips straightened into a hard line. "By yourself? In a storm? Did you tell anyone where you were going, Hallie?" His sapphire eyes pinned the little girl where she stood.

Uh-oh. Hallie's bottom lip began to tremble, and she shifted her gaze to the floor. "You said I could come, remember? When you found me in the orchard crying last month you said if the kids were teasing me bad I could come talk to you."

Even as she felt sorry that some bratty kid had given Hallie a bad time, a warning chill raced up Angie's spine. *The kids.* A funny way for a child to talk about her brothers and sisters.

"What else did I tell you?" Jason asked, sternly.

"To tell Ms. Carmichael, and she would bring me." The little girl's words were a bare whisper and watery with the sound of threatening tears.

The chill spread to Angie's arms and legs. *Ms. Carmichael.* Not Mom. Ms. Carmichael.

"That's right," Jason said. "Have you given any thought to how frightened Ms. Carmichael is right now? How long have you been gone?"

Hallie shook her head, her eyes glued to the tips of her neon yellow boots. "A while. Maybe I should call her."

"Maybe you should. The phone is in here." He turned back to the study, his uneven gait carrying him toward the open door as Hallie followed in snow pants and boots, her step slow and contrite.

Don't ask, Angie warned herself. *Let it go. Just go to your room and stay there for the next three days or three weeks or however long it takes for the plows to get up this damned mountain.*

But she couldn't do it. She had to know. "Is Ms. Carmichael Hallie's mom?'' she called across the foyer to Jason and Hallie's retreating backs.

Jason turned to her, his expression solemn. ''Ms. Carmichael is my headmistress. Hallie's mother and father passed away four years ago. Hallie lives at Kent House with the other children.''

Next to him Hallie's green eyes darkened and she looked off in the corner of the room, as if she was trying very hard not to think about what Jason was saying. Trying very hard not to let the sadness swamp her.

Angie's blood crashed to her toes, her heart twisting in her chest. *An orphan.* That cute, precocious little girl with her green eyes and chubby cheeks and Cupid's lips. An orphan. Lord, she'd hiked up this side of the mountain because she knew she couldn't face those parentless children without wanting to bring them all home. And bringing them home wasn't an option.

Now one of the little darlings was right here, where she could see her Cupid's lips curve into a mischievous smile, hear her little-girl laughter and see the sadness in her eyes when someone spoke of her being alone in the world.

''Are you all right, Angie?'' Jason asked.

His words barely made it through the fog of panic. She forced herself to speak. ''I'm fine. I just have some things I need to do.'' But her voice was thin and reedy and sounded anything but fine.

Jason's brows snapped together in a frown.

She waved him on before he could say anything. ''Go on. Call Ms. Carmichael and take care of Hallie.''

His look was sharp and penetrating. ''I'll do that. And then I'll come check on you.''

She opened her mouth to tell him not to, she wanted to be alone, but he'd already turned his back on her. Putting his hand on Hallie's shoulder, he escorted her into the study. ''We'll call Mrs. Carmichael on my desk phone right now, Hallie. You can assure her you're fine, and tell her you'll be staying with us until the storm is over and the roads are plowed. You're sledding days are over for a while, I'm afraid.''

Chapter Nine

Angie lay on her bed, staring up at the ancient, arched ceiling. It was amazing that eight hundred years ago man could perform such an engineering feat with nothing more than his hands and a few crude tools, while today, with all the technology in the world, he couldn't manage to keep the roads plowed during a little snowstorm.

And she was going to pay dearly for it.

This situation was going to have a bad end. Stuck in this house for the next God-knew-how-many days with Jason and the cute, impetuous little Hallie? Lord, her heart was already tangled up with Jason. The last thing she needed was a cute little girl who would remind her of old dreams and hidden wishes. A cute little girl whom she was going to want to take home with her. A cute little girl whom she would have to leave behind.

Just as she would have to leave Jason behind.

She gave a weary sigh, trying to ignore the tightness

squeezing her chest. How had she gotten herself into this? She should have just refused to do the story on Kent House the minute she was given the assignment.

But she hadn't, she'd gotten on the plane and come up with this harebrained scheme instead. And there was no going back now. The best she could hope for was that she would be the only one to get hurt in this mess.

Three sharp knocks sounded at the door, startling her out of her dark musings. She froze, apprehension racing through her veins. ''Who is it?''

''Who were you expecting?'' Jason asked, as if it couldn't possibly have been anyone else.

Hallie. She'd been afraid it might be Hallie even though Jason had warned her he would check on her. ''No one. I said I had some work to do, remember? I hoped you would leave me in peace to do it.''

''You didn't say anything about work. You said you had 'some things' to do. Which sounded like an excuse to me.''

Maybe if she was quiet, he'd just go away.

''Open the door, Angie.''

Or maybe not. Of course she could refuse to open the door. It was locked and even with a small army he wasn't getting through that heavy, oak monstrosity. But just in case Hallie had followed him upstairs, Angie didn't want to make a scene. She reluctantly pushed herself from the bed, strode across the room, took a deep breath and pulled the door open.

Jason waited patiently on the other side of the oak panel. Alone.

''Where's Hallie?'' she asked, still peeking around, making sure the child wasn't hiding anywhere.

''Down by the fire warming up. I made her a cup of hot cocoa, handed her a couple of cookies and told her to *stay put.*'' He emphasized those last two words with an authoritative jab of his finger.

A tiny smile pulled at her lips. He was obviously not happy that the little sprite hadn't 'stayed put' at Kent House. ''Intrepid little thing, isn't she?''

Jason shot her a disparaging look. ''Intrepid isn't exactly the word I would have picked.''

She wrinkled her nose. ''Probably best I not hear *that* word. Did you give her a lecture?''

Jason ran his fingers through his dark, closely shorn hair, his expression just a little bit harried. ''Right after we called Ms. Carmichael. It was short, curt and to the point.''

Angie chuckled. ''Threatened to kill her if she ever tried anything so stupid again, huh?''

''Anything so *asinine* again,'' he clarified, moving into the room.

She laughed softly. ''If you were scowling then like you are now, I dare say she will treat those words as if they were part of the ten commandments.''

He gave a doubtful grunt as he leaned against the white-and-gold dressing table. ''I can only hope.''

She hid the smile that pulled at her lips. There was just something about Jason Kent's purely male presence in this pink room of little-girl froth and fancy that tickled her.

And then she realized that there was finally someone in the house who would fully appreciate this room of pink confection. ''Hey, Jason, why not put Hallie in here? It won't take me five seconds to move to Dodge.'' She hooked her thumb toward the room decorated in a cowboy motif next door.

He shook his head. ''No, Hallie's not going to run you out. She can stay in Dodge.''

Angie rolled her eyes. "Don't be ridiculous. We're talking a hairbrush and a bottle of red nail polish. It won't take me thirty seconds to move. This room is every little girl's dream. Hallie will think she's in heaven."

He gave her a disparaging look. "I don't want her thinking she's in heaven. Running away the way she did could have had some ugly consequences. I don't think rewarding her is the thing to do."

"Come on, Jason," she coaxed. "You already lectured her about that. Let her have the room."

His mouth hardened in indecision, but finally he gave a single, short nod. "Fine, let her have it." That subject dismissed, his sapphire gaze settled intently on her. "You look better than you did when you left the hall. Feeling better?"

"I told you, I'm fine." Peachy keen if one didn't count the giant bottomless pit yawning before her.

He raised a skeptical brow. "I said you looked better, not rosy-cheeked and bubbly as a mountain spring." His gaze locked onto hers. "What happened downstairs?"

She tipped her head and shot him a quelling look. "Nothing."

He leaned his cane against the dresser and crossed his arms over his chest. "If you want me to believe that, you might want to try erasing the shadows lurking in your eyes."

"Oh, for pity's sake, Jason. If I have shadows in my eyes they're my problem, not yours. Now go away, I've got big-time packing to do." She waved a hand, trying to shoo him out.

He didn't budge. He just leaned against the dresser, his gaze roaming casually over the room as if he were happy to wait all day for her answer if need be. And then his gaze fell on the notebook she'd tossed on the dresser in frustration earlier.

Angie's heart leapt into her throat. She needed to get those pages before he started reading.

But it was too late. Interest sparkling in his eyes, he picked up the notebook, his gaze already skimming the top page.

She crossed the space between them in two giant leaps and tried to snatch the notebook from his hands. "*No. Don't read that!*"

But he just turned sideways, blocking her grasp, his gaze sharpening as he took in the words.

"Jason! Don't—" Too late. She could see the surprise, the anger in his eyes. She backed away, realizing that it was futile to fight him for the notebook now.

He scanned the first page, then flipped to the second, and third, and on and on, his expression getting blacker by the moment. "These aren't notes on Kent House. They're notes on me."

Oh Lord, she would sell her soul to be able to deny it. But the proof was in his hands. "Yes." She closed her eyes against the look of anger and betrayal in those sapphire eyes.

"God, I'm a fool. I wondered the first day you wandered up here if you'd come to ferret out a story. But I dismissed it because of the weather." He shook his head as if he couldn't believe his own stupidity.

He gave her a hard look. "You never intended to do that article on Kent House at all, did you?" His words snapped with accusation.

Her stomach dropped to her toes. This whole mess had started out on a lie. One she had become increasingly uncomfortable with every day. She wasn't going to perpetuate it any longer. She opened her eyes and met his angry gaze. "No, I never planned to do that article. I don't do kids."

"What do you mean, you don't do kids?"

"I just don't do kids. I don't…relate well to them," she finished lamely.

"You don't—" He broke himself off mid-sentence, his hand slicing through the air as if he were too angry to even think about her answer. He narrowed his eyes. "So you came up here with that cock-and-bull story about being an explorer and having gotten lost to get a story on me instead?"

Her cheeks burned with shame. Thinking about it from his point of view made her realize how selfish and thoughtless the action had been. "Something like that, yes." The sorry declaration was a mere whisper.

He pushed away from the dresser, grabbing his cane and stepping into an uneven, angry pace. He turned back to her, his face a mask of disgust. "Well, won't that be a fancy feather in your cap? An exclusive interview with the reclusive Jason Kent."

"I didn't do it for a feather in my cap," she tried desperately to explain.

"Then why *did* you do it?" The question was a low, angry growl.

To protect my heart. But she couldn't say it. The contempt she saw in his eyes now was bad enough. She couldn't stand to pile pity on top of it. She remained silent, letting the silence stretch out.

Suddenly his eyes widened as if he'd finally understood something he'd overlooked in the past. His contempt twisted into an ugly sneer. "God, is that what last night was about for you? Sex in exchange for your story?" An ugly, painful laugh fell from his lips. "Except when the time came, you couldn't make yourself sleep with the cripple after all, could you?''

''No.'' She reached for him. She *couldn't* let him think that. But his angry stare stopped her long before her hands touched him. She dropped them helplessly to her sides. ''That *wasn't* what it was about. I just couldn't face the children—'' She spun away from him, frustration and pain searing through her.

She had to erase that look from his face. The anger at her betrayal. The pain in his eyes when he'd spat the word *cripple*. She spun back to him, splaying her hands in supplication. ''Listen, I don't care about the scar and limp, and I don't care about the damned job anymore, either. I wasn't going to turn the story in to my editor. Even before last night I had decided not to do it.'' Desperation knotted her stomach. He *had* to believe her.

He gave a short, humorless laugh. ''Yeah, right. Save it, Angie. You played me for the fool once. It won't happen again. The kiss last night was nice. But it wasn't *that* nice.'' He turned and strode toward the door, his shoulders stiff, his step more uneven than usual in his haste to get away from her.

His words stabbed like a dagger in her heart. Last night's kiss was as close to heaven as she was going to get in this lifetime. To hear him speak of it with such contempt left a hole in her stomach.

She stared helplessly as he made his way to the door, her mind scrambling for something to say. Something, anything that would make him believe that last night didn't have anything to do with the article. But there was nothing. Nothing she could say that he would believe.

He hesitated at the door, turning to her, his expression hard and demanding. ''Those children deserve your effort, Ms. Rose. Use the article on me if you must. We both know I can't stop you. But talk to Hallie while you're here. Get her story. Get what she knows about the other children and write the Kent House story as a second article. That article might be the one chance they need to find homes. You owe them that.'' His eyes narrowed to tiny sapphire bands. ''You owe *me* that.'' Without another word he slammed out of the room.

Angie stared at the closed portal, a second dagger plunging next to the first. She closed her eyes and struggled to breathe. She'd been so wrapped up in her own selfish attempt to protect her heart that she'd been blind to the fact that not writing the article could hurt the children.

Jason was right. She owed the kids. What she owed Jason she would never be able to repay, but she could write the article on Kent House. A great article. One that would have prospective parents lined up at its gates.

But not now. Not now. With shaking hands, she picked up her hairbrush and the small, red bottle of nail polish from the dressing table and dropped them in her purse. Now she just needed to move into the room next door and crawl into the bed and pull the blanket with its cowboys and Indians up over her head and...cry.

Angie stood at the sink in the bathroom, the cold water running into her hands. She scooped up the cool liquid and raised it to her face. Her eyes were in pretty good shape, actually. She'd cried herself out hours ago. But the bracing effect of the cool water was helping to push away the numbing fog of despair that had gripped her when Jason had slammed out of her room.

She drenched her face a couple more times, then snatched up the face towel hanging next to the sink. Burying her face in its deep folds, she savored her last few moments of peace and garnered her strength. She was about to head down and start her interview with Hallie. Her stomach tightened at the thought, but she ignored it. She had to do this.

With a final deep breath she tossed the towel aside and headed back to her new room to collect her notebook and pen. She scooped them off the bed and started downstairs. At least she'd destroyed the pages on Jason hours ago so she wouldn't have to look at the incriminating notes again.

Another wave of regret washed over her. If only she'd destroyed them when she'd first had qualms about the article. But she hadn't. And now it was too late. The damage was done.

Making her feet move down the stone stairs, she tried to ignore the hall's chill as she looked across the foyer at the closed study doors. Jason and Hallie were probably in there. With lunch long since over and dinner a good hour off, Angie couldn't imagine where else they would be. She knew Jason hadn't shown the little girl to her room because she hadn't heard them. And with the shutters closed, Jason's office wasn't very child-friendly, but she could easily imagine them snuggled down in the study enjoying the fire.

She stopped in front of the large, sliding doors, her stomach clenching and her hands strangling the notebook and pen. She didn't want to face Jason again, didn't want to see the contempt on his face—the contempt and the anger of betrayal. But she couldn't put it off forever.

She took another deep, fortifying breath, slid one of the giant doors open, slipped inside and pulled it closed behind her. The cheery warmth of the fire enveloped her immediately, but it didn't calm her nerves. Not with the dark, brooding look Jason leveled on her from across the room.

Obviously the last few hours hadn't calmed his anger one bit. He made no move to greet her, not even a small nod of his head. He just sat in his large wing chair next to the fire, his fingers tapping a slow, uneasy tattoo on the chair's arms, his lips compressed into a hard line.

Angie swallowed hard, resisting the urge to wipe her sweaty palms on her jeans, and turned her attention to Hallie.

The little girl looked up at her with a welcoming smile from where she lounged on her tummy in front of the fire, drawing on a piece of paper with a red marker. "Hi. Jason said you were in your room because you didn't feel good. Are you better now?"

Angie forced her own lips into a smile. "Yeah. I see you managed to dry out while I was gone." She also noticed how tiny the young girl seemed without her winter gear. She was so delicate that she seemed more like a mythical wraith than a girl of flesh and blood. And to complete the wood-nymph look, a riot of shiny black curls tumbled in wild disarray around the small oval face and tiny shoulders.

Hallie swung up into a sitting position, kicking her legs out in front of her and wiggling her toes. "My socks never dried, but Jason's socks are better anyway."

Angie looked at the pair of white gym socks encasing Hallie's feet. And legs. Pulled over navy leggings, the soft cotton reached beyond her knees. A smile pulled at Angie's lips. "They look warm and snuggly."

Hallie giggled. "Yeah. Jason says I can take them back to Kent House with me."

The little girl obviously thought the socks were quite a prize. "That was nice of him. And speaking of Kent House, did he tell you I wanted to talk to you about it?"

Hallie pulled the picture she'd been drawing earlier into her lap. "No."

Angie looked at Jason and raised a questioning brow.

He stared back, his hard gaze unwavering. "I wasn't sure you would, with your 'relating' problem and all."

She took the prick, ignoring the tiny flow of blood. She'd hurt him. She owed him a few free shots. Forcing the smile back on her face, she looked at Hallie. "Well, I guess he didn't tell you I was a reporter, either, huh?"

"What's a 'porter?" Hallie asked, setting to work on her picture again.

Angie glanced quickly around the room. Spying a magazine on the coffee table, she picked it up, walked over to Hallie and handed it down to her. "Someone who writes stories about people and things and then puts those stories in a book like this."

Her small hands clutching the shiny pages, Hallie glanced at the magazine. After a quick perusal she looked up, her green eyes sparkling. "Yeah? Will the story be about me?"

"About you and the other children at Kent House."

Hallie's eyes got brighter. "Cool. Can we put a unicorn in it?"

Angie laughed. "Maybe. First I need to find out some things about you, though."

"What do you want to know?" Hallie's expression turned very serious, as if she were intent on getting the work out of the way so she could get on to the fun stuff. That unicorn.

Repressing her smile, Angie dropped down onto the floor in front of Hallie, crossed her legs and propped her notebook on her knee. "Let's start with the simple stuff. How old are you?"

"Six."

"What's your favorite color?"

"Pink."

Angie smiled at the answer. Hallie was going to love that room. "And I'll bet your favorite animal is a unicorn, huh?" Angie asked with a teasing smile.

Hallie nodded enthusiastically. "I have them hanging on my wall in my room."

Angie lifted a brow. "Really? Do you have your own room at Kent House?"

The little girl shook her head. "I did for a while when I first came, but I didn't like it. It's scary alone. So when Camilla came they put her in with me."

"That was nice."

Hallie nodded, her attention back on the page stretched out on her small legs. "Yeah. She likes unicorns, too."

"That's good." Unfortunately, she needed to move the interview on to more important issues. She gave the little girl a warm smile. "How do you like living at Kent House?"

"It's okay, when the boys aren't teasing me. But I don't have a mom and dad." A flash of anger skated across the little girl's face. "If I had a mom and dad, the boys wouldn't ever tease me."

Angie's heart flinched. Hallie's escape this morning hadn't been about the naughty boys. It had been about feeling alone. About feeling as if no one was really in her corner. "I hate to tell you this, kid," Angie said gently. "But having a mom and dad won't save you from the boys. Just ask me. I had a mom and dad, and my two older brothers teased me and my sister mercilessly."

Interest sparkled in Hallie's eyes. "Yeah? Even with your mom and dad there?"

"Yep, even so."

Hallie's expression became thoughtful, maybe a little

sad. "Well, a mom and dad would still be nice, don't you think?"

Angie cleared her throat, trying to loosen the knot tightening there. "Yeah, moms and dads are good." *Every little girl should have one of each.*

Hallie nodded, once again wielding her red pen with bold panache. "I think so, too, but until they fixed it, I had a sick heart, so Ms. Carmichael says we have to find just the right parents for me."

She'd wondered why a child as bright and beautiful as Hallie was at Kent House. Now she knew. "Just the right parents" was a nice way of saying parents that wouldn't be afraid of adopting a child with a history of heart problems. Parents who weren't afraid of the possible doctor bills a serious health problem like heart disease could incur.

Angie stared at the little girl with her rosy cheeks and Cupid's lips and green eyes, all framed by those wild, black curls. *Your heart wouldn't scare me away, Hallie. If I could, I would take you home and love you until you forgot you'd ever been alone.* But the thought was wasted. She couldn't take the little girl home. What she *could* do was write a great article and hope to God a pair of loving parents would step up to the plate.

To do that she needed to paint a picture of Hallie that people couldn't resist. "So tell me, Hallie, besides sneaking out of the house to go *sledding,*" she emphasized the word with a conspiratorial wink, "what do you like to do?"

Hallie giggled at the allusion to her running away. "I like the zoo."

"Yeah? I like the zoo, too. What's your favorite animal there?"

"Well, Camilla likes the monkeys the best, but I like the yaks."

Angie raised a brow. "The yaks?"

Hallie nodded solemnly. "They're sad."

"Why are they sad?"

"I think they're lonely. Everybody is always at the monkey cage, and nobody's ever at the yak cage. I asked Ms. Carmichael if we could bring them home, but she says no. So when I'm at the zoo I spend most of my time with them."

Hallie had a bad heart and no parents, but she was worried about the yaks at the zoo. Angie's heart contracted again. "Well, I'll tell ya what, kid. Next time I go to the zoo I will definitely spend some time with the yaks. In the meantime, why don't you tell me a little about you?"

"Like what?"

"Hmm. Like what you want to be when you grow up."

Hallie looked up from her drawing with a teasing grin. "Maybe a 'porter."

Angie laughed. "Yeah, that's what we need, little squirt reporters. How about an artist? What are you drawing there?"

"It was going to be a butterfly, but now it's a unicorn for the story. I'll show you." The little girl grabbed the picture, scrambled over on hands and knees and crawled into Angie's lap.

Angie froze, her breath catching in her throat as Hallie snuggled into her lap like a baby bird settling into its nest. Her sharp little elbow poked Angie in the side; her tiny shoulders leaned against her chest.

Panic and yearning crashed through Angie. Part of her wanted to set the little girl aside and run while the running was good. But the other part of her wanted to wrap her arms around Hallie and hang on tight.

"See?" Hallie held the picture up in front of them so Angie could see.

"Yeah—" Her throat was so tight she sounded as if a noose were wrapped around her neck. She cleared her voice and tried again. "Yeah. He's very nice. I particularly like the butterfly wings here on his rump." She pointed to what remained of the original creation.

Hallie giggled again, wiggling in her lap. "Pretend that's not there."

Before she could stop herself, Angie settled her hands on Hallie's hips and pulled her a little closer. Just to keep her still, she told herself. But it was a lie, and she knew it. She wanted to hold her. Wanted to wrap her body around the little girl like mothers did around the world. Wanted to wrap her up and protect her and comfort her and share a moment of innocent communion. "Okay. The wings aren't there. In that case he's perfect."

"Is it good enough I could be an artist?"

"Oh definitely."

"Good enough to be in the book?"

"I think I can arrange that." She would twist the art director's arm if she had to. Hallie would see her creation in eight-by-ten glossy.

Putting the drawing back in her lap, Hallie glanced up at Angie. "What about you? Did you always want to be a 'porter when you grew up?"

Angie's heart clenched. With this little child in her lap, it had never been more plain to her what she'd wanted to be when she grew up. Sadness slid through her like dark shadows claiming the night. "No, actually, it was just something I fell into one day."

Hallie's eyes popped wide. "You *fell* into it?"

Angie smiled at Hallie's literal translation. "It's just an expression. It means when I was looking for a job there just happened to be an opening for a reporter, and I took it. Although my mother will tell you I'm so nosy I was a natural for the job."

Hallie giggled at that. "If you didn't want to be a 'porter, what did you want to be?"

Angie tightened her grip on Hallie, savoring the feel of the tiny body snuggled against hers. *A wife and mother.* "I don't remember. It was a long time ago."

"Didn't you want to get married?" Hallie asked, adding small, puffy clouds to the unicorn picture.

"I was going to marry a man once. But it didn't work out."

"Why not?"

I had an accident, and he didn't love me anymore. "We just decided we'd be better off single, I guess."

"He decided? Or you?"

He did. "We both thought it would be best."

Hallie looked up from her drawing and peered over her shoulder at Angie, her gaze oddly intense for a six-year-old. "No, you look sad. I think he left."

At first the girl's perception surprised Angie, but then she thought about Hallie's life. Losing her parents at such a young age. Living in a group home. Heart problems. The little girl probably knew more about sadness and what caused it than Angie did. "Maybe I couldn't give him what he wanted."

"What did he want?"

Angie's eyes stung, a single tear spilling over her lower lid before she could stop it. She flicked it away quickly as if she were just scratching an itch and concentrated on keeping the tears from her voice. "Oh, I don't know. You'd have to ask him, I guess."

Trying to pull herself together, she drew a steadying breath as she looked up and away from Hallie and the red unicorn. And straight into Jason's intense gaze.

He was still staring at her, his expression just as hard as when she'd first come in. But where there had been simmering anger in those sapphire eyes earlier, now there seemed to be...speculation.

A warning chill ran through her. She didn't know what that look was about, but it couldn't be good. And she was definitely not up to another round of...anything with Jason.

She gently lifted Hallie from her lap. "Listen kiddo, I need to get upstairs and start working on this story. You finish your picture and I'll get it from you a little later, okay?"

Hallie nodded, flopping back on her stomach and going to work on more clouds.

Angie stared at the curly-haired imp with her small fingers wrapped intently around the giant red marker and the tip of her tongue stuck out between her lips. Her arms suddenly ached with emptiness, and the skin that had been warmed by Hallie only moments before felt chilled. Clutching her notebook and pen, she fled the room, feeling Jason's penetrating stare every step of the way.

Jason watched Angie flee the study. When he had stormed out of her room this morning he'd been positive she had played him for a sucker, but now...he wasn't so sure.

When he'd found the notes on her article she had said she didn't "do kids." Didn't "relate" to them. But further into the argument she had claimed that she couldn't "*face* the children." At the time that statement had sounded as lame as the first two excuses. But now...

He'd seen a lot of longing in the faces of prospective parents since he'd opened Kent House. But he'd never seen longing as deep or pain-filled as that which he'd seen on Angie's face when she was holding Hallie in her lap. And now that he thought about it, it wasn't the first time he'd seen Angie react strongly when the subject of kids was mentioned.

She had turned pale as a ghost and lost her appetite when he'd explained why he'd decorated the pink room as he had. And she'd turned almost as pale this morning when she'd learned that Hallie was an orphan, not a neighbor kid with two living parents.

Maybe she *was* afraid of facing a roomful of homeless children. But did that really make sense? If she wanted a child, why didn't she just have one? Except...

Steven.

Another part of the puzzle that he'd spent a good part of the day trying to understand suddenly seemed to slip into place. The kisses. He'd been sitting here most of the afternoon, staring at the fire, trying to tell himself that last night's kisses had just been part of Angie's attempt to get her story. But even with the anger burning in his gut, he hadn't been able to convince himself. They had felt real.

Both the kisses and her passion. And now, with Steven in the picture, the words she'd said as she'd run away from him maybe made some kind of sense. Her words echoed in his head again.

You deserve more. And when you realize I can't give you more, you'll leave me behind.

Did Angie think every man would leave her because that worm Steven had? And if she was foolish enough to believe that, would she take the next illogical leap and

think that without a man there would be no children in
her future?

It was a thought. Certainly one worth checking out.
Because if those kisses had been real, if her passion had
been real, he'd be a fool to walk away.

Chapter Ten

Jason headed up the stairs, his cane in one hand and a plate with a chicken sandwich in the other. After her interview with Hallie this afternoon, Angie had skipped dinner to hide in her room. Actually, Angie had chosen to do her hiding in the bathroom since he'd brought Hallie upstairs and started reading her a bedtime story. Just another indication that Angie was having a hard time being around the charming Hallie.

But hiding wasn't going to save her from him. He had questions to ask, and a closed door wasn't going to stop him. He glanced down the hall at the bathroom door. Still shut. Despite the fact that he'd left Hallie sound asleep half an hour ago, Angie still hadn't found the nerve to come out of the bathroom.

He walked down the hall and rapped quietly on the oak panel. ''You can come out now. Hallie's asleep.''

Silence greeted him from the other side of the door.

"You can't hide in there for the next five or six days, Angie, you might as well come out now."

The door opened with a whoosh. "I'm not hiding." Her protest was adamant, but her look was wary.

He felt no compunction to reassure her. He was still trying to decide whether he should be angry with her or not. "Really? You've been in here for over an hour and a half. Even for a woman who loves to wallow in the bathroom, a trait I hadn't noticed in you up until now, that seems a little excessive."

She pointedly ignored his comment, her wary gaze dropping to the sandwich. "Is that for me?"

"You missed dinner. I thought you might be hungry."

She raised her gaze to his. "Is it laced with strychnine?"

"Rat poisoning. Strychnine works too quickly, and I have some questions I want to ask. With rat poisoning, which takes several doses to do its dirty deed, I can ask my questions and decide later if I want to finish you off or not."

She gave him a quelling look. "Very funny."

"Sorry, I'm not in a comedic mood," he admitted, handing her the plate.

She gave a weary, frustrated sigh as she accepted the sandwich and set it on a nearby plant stand. "No, I imagine you're not. Look, Jason, I'm sorry. I should never even have contemplated doing a story on you. I should just have told my editor right off the bat that I couldn't do the story she'd assigned."

"Yes, you should have. But that's a moot point. You're here. What I want to know now is why you couldn't face the children at Kent House. And why you ran away from our kiss the other night."

She went utterly still, like a rabbit who'd just caught

sight of a wolf and wondered if the predator had actually seen her. "I told you this morning. I just overreacted last night. There's no more to it than that."

"I think there's a lot more to it than that."

Worry creased her brow, but she tried to play it cool, shrugging a shoulder. "I can't stop you from thinking, Jason."

"You want to know why I think you ran away?"

"More than life itself."

He smiled at the dry announcement, despite the tension crackling between them. "I think you ran away because you're afraid of getting left again. I think Steven hurt you badly enough that you've decided that getting involved with any man isn't worth the risk. And I think you've somehow tied that nonsense up with the idea of parenthood. As in, you think if you don't do the relationship thing you can't do the kid thing, either. And you want kids, Angie. I saw the longing in your face when Hallie was sitting in your lap."

Panic exploded in her eyes and she spun away from him, dashing into the bathroom. "You don't know what you're talking about."

Her reaction clearly told him he knew exactly what he was talking about. He gentled his voice. "Listen, I don't know what kind of number Steven did on you. But all men aren't creeps who—"

"Stop it. Steven wasn't a creep," she tried to explain, turning back to him, her voice desperate to make him understand. "He was a loving, decent man who just…" She closed her eyes as if searching for the right words.

"Left you standing at the altar," he pointed out sharply, angry that she would defend a man who had obviously caused her so much pain. Was still causing her pain.

A deep, aching sorrow filled her expression. "He had his reasons." The words were a bare whisper.

"I'd love to hear them."

She shook her head frantically, the scared rabbit once again. "They're not important."

Frustration clawed at his gut. She wasn't going to give anything up voluntarily. "Then I'll just have to assume Steven is a cowardly bastard."

"Stop talking about him that way," she snapped. "You don't know anything about him."

He knew enough to know he didn't like the man. "Fine. The man was a bloody saint. He was all that was good and wonderful. Which is why, of course, you've sworn off men for life."

She narrowed her eyes to tiny hazel lasers. "Leave it alone, Jason. You don't know what you're talking about."

"Of course I don't. You won't *tell* me anything." He gritted his teeth and resisted the urge to reach over and strangle her.

"There is nothing to tell," she spat back, her own temper matching his.

"Yeah, right," he muttered, wanting to kill someone. Preferably the invertebrate marvel Steven. "All I'm saying is that just because you didn't have whatever Steven wanted or needed, doesn't mean any other man on the planet would share his feelings."

She shook her head, pain once again shadowing her eyes. "Like I said, you don't know what you're talking about."

"Well, let me tell you what I *do* know. I know the kiss we shared curled your pretty little toes. I won't tell you what it did to me. That would have you blushing right down to those sexy, red toenails. But I will say that considering how well that kiss went, maybe it's time you rethought your policy on men. At least on one man," he qualified, because the thought of her rethinking it about anyone but him set his teeth on edge.

"But—"

"And I also know that when you look at Hallie there is a sadness and wanting so deep in your eyes it must hurt like hell. And there is no reason for it. If you're under some false impression that you can't have kids just because you don't plan on having a man, maybe you ought to rethink your policy on kids, too—even if you don't rethink your position on men. Agencies adopt to single parent homes all the time these days."

She clenched her fists and drew a deep, steadying breath as if she were garnering her strength and curbing her temper all at once. "Look, Jason. Last night's kiss was wonderful. But that's all it was. A single kiss. Beyond that moment it had no future. As for the rest, don't tell me how to live my life."

"Why not? You don't have any problem telling me how to live mine—"

"It's not the same."

"It's the same, babe. And the kiss *is* my business. As for it not having a future? You a fortune teller now?"

She sent him a withering glance.

Which he completely ignored. "You better rethink your career choices, too, if you think you are. Because I've got to tell you, lady, what happened between us in the study sure as hell felt like it had a future to me. And someone sure as hell should tell you how to live your life, because all you're doing is hiding from it."

"*I'm* hiding?" Outraged indignation filled her voice. "Don't you *dare* tell me I'm hiding. My life may not be exactly what I thought it would be, but I've made my peace and moved on. Which is a heck of a lot more than

you can say. Have you even stuck so much as your big
toe out of this house in the last three years?''

She didn't give him a chance to reply, she just kept
talking, her finger jabbing the air. ''No, you haven't. So
don't lecture me on how to live my life while you're
hiding your sorry butt up here in your own private poor-
poor-pitiful-me kingdom. If you're looking for someone's
life to fix, *fix your own.*'' She shoved past him and
stormed up the hall to her room.

He let her go, his gut clenching as if he'd just taken a
sucker punch, his hand strangling the eagle at the top of
his cane. They weren't talking about him, damn it. They
were talking about her.

And it was *not* the same thing. There was nothing
wrong with her. She was a beautiful, vibrant, healthy
woman. Not a cripple who needed a cane to get from one
point to another. Or a scarred monster who sent children
running.

*Hallie didn't go running. In fact she ran to you, not
away from you.*

The *last* opinion he wanted to hear right now. But no
matter how much he tried to ignore it, the incessant voice
droned on.

*Hallie's not afraid of you. She doesn't think you're a
monster.*

What does Hallie have to do with this?

Just pointing out that Angie might have a point.

Which point would that be?

*That you very well might have wasted the last three
years of your life hiding up here.*

Don't be ridiculous. People *are* afraid of me.

*But they could get used to you. Hallie did. You just
don't like the adjustment period because it bruises your
ego.*

And my heart.

Is your heart doing any better hiding here in this god-forsaken pile of rocks?

Yes.

Liar.

All right, maybe not. But at least I have my pride.

Well, we both know that will keep you warm at night.

Shut up.

You would like to be warm at night wouldn't you?

I'm plenty warm now.

But you're lonely.

So what? Another ten years, I'll adjust.

No you won't. You'll go mad.

Maybe.

Angie's just afraid, you know. Steven obviously hurt her badly.

Yes. He clenched his fists wishing the man was in the room with him right now. He couldn't force Angie to tell him what had gone wrong with their relationship, but he'd have no compunction about beating the answers he wanted from Steven. Not when he thought about the shadows that never seemed far from Angie's eyes.

So what are you going to do about it?

He stared at Angie's closed bedroom door with a wry smile. I don't know.

You'd better give it some thought if you want another kiss.

I want more than a kiss.

How much more?

I don't know.

Well, you'd best think about it. Time is short. And I'd recommend trashing the poor-poor-pitiful-me routine. The lady's clearly not impressed.

He stared harder at the closed door that led to Dodge.
I'll think about it.

Angie straightened the sheets on Hallie's bed and then
pulled the pink comforter up. Since Jason and Hallie had
headed downstairs early this morning, and she hadn't
heard a peep from them since, she figured it was safe do
a little cleaning up. And even housework was preferable
to agonizing over the giant mess she'd made of things.

But no matter how hard she tried to divert her thoughts
she couldn't shake the feeling of impending disaster.
She'd known when Steven had left her at the altar that
she wasn't ever going to be able to fulfill a man's dreams.
And she'd decided right then and there never to give another man the chance to find her wanting. So she'd made
a rule, a rule that would allow her to live a simple life
with no risk to either her mental well-being or her heart.

No more men.

It was a simple rule.

So what in the *hell* had possessed her to break it with
Jason Kent?

Sighing wearily, she gave the comforter a final, impatient tug. She knew why she'd broken the rule. Yes, she'd
built a good life for herself. She had a good job that was
challenging and paid well. She had a lovely little apartment to come home to when she wasn't working on a
story. She had a family who loved her—a mother and
father who supported her in whatever she did, brothers
and sisters who checked in on her and shared their children with her. But it just wasn't the same as having a
family of her own. It certainly wasn't the same as having
a man by her side.

Jason had made her blood rush through her veins and
her stomach flip in feminine delight. Made her yearn to

feel those long, strong fingers against her skin. Made her ache to be held in his arms.

And she had thought she was safe.

It was just *one* date. One night to enjoy a warm fire and handsome man's company and a glass of champagne. But somehow everything had gotten out of hand.

More specifically, the kiss had gotten out of hand. It was supposed to have been an easy, friendly kiss. But the minute his lips had touched hers the world had caught on fire, with need and want and raw sexual chemistry feeding the flames.

And then Hallie had shown up the next morning—another sharp reminder of what she'd been missing in life—and everything had spiraled down from there until Jason had figured it all out.

Well, not all of it. He thought Steven had done something to scare her away from men and the whole dating relationship thing. He didn't know it was her deficiency that had made Steven walk away. Nor did he understand that children weren't an option for her even with today's easier adoption policies. And Lord, she didn't want him to know.

The desire she saw in his eyes, his obvious wish to have more come of their relationship was like a balm to her aching spirit. But letting anything more develop between them could lead to Jason finding out why Steven had left her, and that would be disastrous.

Which is exactly why she'd avoided him since their little confrontation last night, why she'd been sneaking down to grab something to eat only when she knew Jason and Hallie wouldn't be in the kitchen.

The only problem was that she had a passel full of questions she needed to ask Jason to complete her story on Kent House, and she had yet to figure out a method of getting those answers without talking to him.

She glanced at her watch. Four o'clock. Jason and Hallie were probably in the study, enjoying the fire right now. And she couldn't put off this interview forever. She quickly picked up the half-dozen throw pillows Hallie had knocked on the floor and tossed them back on the bed. Returning to her room, she grabbed her pen and notebook and headed down to the study.

Stepping into the warm room she found Hallie studiously working on something at Jason's desk. But Jason was nowhere to be found. She walked over to the little girl. "Hey, Hallie. Whatcha doing?"

"Colorin'. Jason said he had to do some work and I should stay here and color. You want to color with me?"

Angie looked down at the swarm of giant bumblebees Jason had drawn on his blotter for Hallie to color. Her heart clenched in her chest. She loved to color with her nieces and nephews.

But coloring with Hallie would be a mistake.

The fragile little girl offered as much emotional danger as Jason did. "No thanks, sweetie. I need to work, too. I have some questions to ask Jason." But she couldn't keep from running her hand over Hallie's tiny head, feeling the springy, silky texture of all those wild curls.

Hallie nodded, coloring in a fat stripe with a green marker. "Okay, maybe after."

"Maybe." But it was a lie. Jason could answer all the questions she had left, and the more time she spent alone, the safer she was going to be. On all fronts. She tucked a particularly wayward curl behind Hallie's ear. "Is Jason in his office?"

Hallie nodded, her concentration focused on the next stripe.

"Okay. Color well." She slipped out of the study, her heart feeling as if a giant stone were crushing it. She *wanted* to stay and color with Hallie. Wanted to wrap the little girl in her arms and never let her go. But wanting it didn't make it wise.

Ruthlessly squelching the desolate feeling, she crossed the foyer to Jason's office. The one thing she could do for Hallie was to write an article that would have prospective parents lined up around this mountain. At Jason's office she knocked once, took a deep breath and went in.

With the shutters closed over the stained glass windows, the room was once again suffused with flickering light. Sitting in his chair in front of the computer bank, Jason swiveled around to face her. He casually propped one ankle on the opposite knee, leaned back in his chair and cocked a single, teasing brow. "Finally decide you couldn't stand one more minute of being alone?"

She glanced over his shoulders at his computers, then gave him a sweet smile. "Busy losing another bundle?"

The smile he shot her was uncomfortably smug. "Actually I was searching real estate sites trying to find a suitable location for another group home like Kent House."

Surprise zipped through her. "You're kidding?"

He shook his head. "Nope."

The thought of Jason breaking out of his self-imposed prison thrilled her. She couldn't stop the thought that she had helped precipitate his decision. A trill of righteous triumph bubbled through her veins.

She gave him a cheeky smile. "What? You finally figure out I was right about you sitting up here on your mountain crying in your beer too long?"

He shot her a disparaging look. "Don't let your head swell too much. Nothing has happened yet. And nothing might be the end result. A lot depends on the kids at Kent House. After the storm I'll start going back over there, re-introduce myself to the kids. If they adjust to this face, I'll open another house. If they don't…''

It would be tough going at first, she knew. The children probably would react negatively to the scar in the begin-ning. But they would soon adjust, she was sure of it. And then the joy and satisfaction Jason would get out of the children and the work would be its own reward. She couldn't stop the sappy smile that turned her lips. ''Good for you.''

''Don't give me too much credit. My motive to 'quit crying in my beer,' as you so eloquently put it, is far from pure.'' His lips twisted ruefully. ''In fact it's as self-serving as hell.''

She raised a brow. ''How do you figure?''

He gave a careless shrug. ''As you can imagine, I had a lot to think about last night after our little skirmish. After I got over my initial urge to strangle you—a desire that passed quicker than I would have expected, actu-ally—I thought maybe there was some merit to your ar-gument. Maybe I *had* wasted a lot of time wallowing in self-pity.''

He locked his gaze onto hers with bold directness. ''But mostly I thought about you. About you and how much I wanted you. And it occurred to me that since you were already tossing enough obstacles between us all by your-self, I didn't need to be adding any more hurdles to the field. And since you seemed to think I shouldn't be push-ing you to make changes in your life as long as I have issues of my own, I thought I would just take that obstacle out of play.''

Her stomach flipped and her pulse raced at his decla-ration, a declaration that thrilled the woman in her, even as the threat of disaster clamored up her spine. She should put a stop to this right now. Tell him his efforts were useless. But all she could think about was that he'd spent the night thinking of ways to get close to her. She swallowed hard and tried not to sound breathless as she spoke. "I see you've thought a lot about this."

"All night long." His voice was low, seductive, making it clear he'd spent the night not only thinking about chasing her but of catching her as well.

Her pulse raced harder, want and longing throbbing through her, but wanting and longing didn't change the fact that she couldn't give him what he wanted. Nothing changed that reality. And now that he'd made this first step to getting his life back on track, it would be only a matter of time before he realized that his dream was still within his grasp.

A dream she couldn't give him. She drew a slow, steadying breath and desperately tried to reason with him. "Don't start this, Jason. It has no future."

A frown wrinkled his brow. "You worry too much about the future. Why can't you just think about the here and now?"

"For a man who's happy with the here and now, you certainly wanted answers to an awful lot of questions last night."

He studied her, his expression intent. "I don't like the shadows in your eyes. I want to chase them away, but if you don't tell me what causes them, I can't."

"You can't anyway." No one could.

"Then let me soothe them. Today, if not tomorrow."

She closed her eyes against the tantalizing offer. Against the naked desire in his eyes. "Don't."

"Why?"

Because I want it as much as you do and I don't know

if I can hold out against a siege. "Because it's just…impossible." She spun back to the door, intent on leaving before he could batter at her defenses any more. The questions for the story would have to wait.

"What if I promise not to ask any questions?"

She froze, her fingers strangling the heavy brass knob, her breath catching in her throat.

"Come to me tonight," he coaxed quietly. "Come to me and let me show you with my hands and my mouth and my body how to forget that the future is even out there."

Her stomach clenched. No matter how much she wanted it, she'd be a fool to go to him. In a thousand different ways. Because she would open herself up to discovery. Because she would hurt him if he decided he wanted more and she couldn't give it. Because she would only miss him more when she had to leave. "I can't."

"Yes, you can. I promise not to ask any questions. Or ask for more than you can give."

She closed her eyes against the seductive invitation. Closed her eyes and prayed for…what? Strength? Deliverance? A desperate laugh echoed through her head. Both. The question was, the strength to say what? No? Or yes? And deliverance where? Out of his arms? Or into them?

"Think about it."

"I'll think about it," she whispered and slipped out the door, yearning twisting through her veins, caution pounding in her heart.

Chapter Eleven

Jason handed Hallie the measuring cup full of milk. "Pour that into the bowl with the flour and eggs."

Standing on the chair he'd dragged over from the table, Hallie carefully tipped the milk into the metal bowl, her mouth screwed into an unhappy pout. "Ms. Carmichael just pours the milk right from the carton. And she uses a *real* pancake mix. Out of a box. She doesn't make it up."

Hallie was one of his all-time favorite kids at Kent House, but this morning he wasn't up to dealing with anyone. He shot the little complainer a sideways glance. "We're not making it up. We're using a recipe. And these pancakes will be better than the ones that come out of a box." And she ought to be happy he'd agreed to make the things in the first place. After the night he'd had, making pancakes had not been at the top of the list of things he wanted to do this morning. Sleep had been at the top of that list. Or ignoring his more civilized instincts and crashing down Angie's door, dragging her off to a remote part of the castle and giving them both what they wanted, but what Angie was too stubborn to take.

"Who says they'll be better?" Hallie asked, picking up the wooden spoon and giving the ingredients an awkward stir that sent a little puff of flour into the air.

Who indeed? For all he knew the bloody things would be inedible. He'd never made pancakes before, and he'd discovered in the past that using a recipe didn't necessarily ensure culinary success. "Just keep stirring while I get out the griddle. If you don't like the pancakes, you can always wait till lunch to eat."

Hallie whipped her head toward him, giving an open-mouthed look of such appalled horror that she should have been given an Academy award for it.

"Don't look at me like that, just stir the pancakes."

"Boy, are you a crabby cake this morning," she said in perfect imitation of Ms. Carmichael as she sent the spoon swirling again.

Yes, he was. And his mood wasn't likely to change. It had been a damned long night. He'd been too hopeful—too horny—to sleep as he'd waited fruitlessly for Angie to show up. And when he'd heard Hallie's bedroom door open this morning at precisely five-thirty—like she had reveille or something—he'd known he wasn't going to get any sleep this morning, either.

And *then,* when he'd joined the little monster downstairs in the kitchen, she'd turned up her nose at every cereal box he'd produced, refused to eat anything he could cook and had demanded pancakes instead. And she was still giving him grief.

He pointed to the silver bowl. "Stir the pancakes, Hallie." He snatched up his cane and moved to the cabinet that held the griddle. Just as he was pulling it out, he heard the kitchen door swing open.

Angie.

He straightened, turning toward the door.

Hovering in the doorway, she looked as tired as he was. Good. He'd waited half the night, hoping she'd see through her problems, whatever they were, and come to him. When she hadn't shown up by two o'clock he'd figured she wasn't coming, despite the fact that he knew she wanted to. So he'd spent what was left of the night trying to ignore the need that would not quit pounding through his veins. If she'd been in her room the whole time sleeping like a baby, it would really have gotten his goat. But it looked as if her night had been as hard as his.

Apprehension shadowed her eyes now as she stood across the room watching Hallie, debating no doubt whether she should come in and join them or not.

He mentally shook his head. He could see her fear of getting too attached to the little girl—a fear he was in no mood to tolerate this morning. "Come on in, Angie. You can help with breakfast."

She started at the sound of his voice, her gaze flying to his. Her brows crumpled into a quick scowl when she saw his unrepentant grin, but she forced a wooden smile to her lips and moved into the kitchen.

Instead of joining them in the stove area, she stopped on the other side of the counter and leaned over to peer into Hallie's mixing bowl. "Breakfast?"

Hallie nodded enthusiastically.

"Hmm. What is it?"

"Pancakes," Hallie announced cheerfully. "Animal pancakes."

Jason whipped his attention from Angie and settled his gaze on the little stirrer. "Animal pancakes?"

Hallie nodded. "Yeah. Ms. Carmichael reads us a book where the mom makes animal pancakes for her kids. But Ms. Carmichael won't make them. She says with fifteen kids to feed it's hard enough to make regular pancakes and keep them warm. But since there's only three of us, we could do animal pancakes, don'tcha think?"

Jason's heart clenched. He remembered reading stories when he was young, too, stories about little boys with moms and dads. He remembered lying in bed dreaming about having his own parents some day. Ones that would do special things for him like the parents in the books always did for their little boys. Things like throwing a football back and forth on a Saturday afternoon, or making window ornaments for Halloween.

Or making animal pancakes.

He cleared the tightness in his throat and nodded. "Okay, animal pancakes it is." He didn't have the first clue how to make the things, but if Hallie wanted animal pancakes, he could certainly stop being grouchy long enough to help her make them.

"I can't wait to see this," Angie said, with a knowing lift of her brows, her trepidation momentarily slipping away as she anticipated the culinary mess he was about to wade into.

He scowled at her, putting the griddle on the stove and flipping on the gas flame beneath it. "Feeling safe over on your side of the counter, are you?"

Her apprehension slid back into place, but she did her best to hide it behind a practiced shrug. "Don't be silly. It's just too crowded back there for three."

Uh-huh. There was enough room on this side of the kitchen for ten cooks and an equal number of assistants. She was just trying to keep her distance from Hallie. Trying to protect herself.

Not that he didn't understand the sentiment. Lord knows he'd protected himself with voracious zeal over the last three years. And even now the idea of facing the outside world tied his gut in knots. The thought of putting himself out there when complete rejection and humiliation might well be the only result practically paralyzed him with fear. But now that Angie had pushed him this far, he realized that he could either take the risk or slowly go mad up here on this mountain without ever having tried to save himself at all.

He wasn't ready for that surrender yet.

And since Angie was responsible for pushing him to this point, he saw no good reason to let her hide behind her fears either, particularly when what she was hiding from was a little girl as sweet as Hallie.

He looked over his shoulder at his midget cook. "Should we leave her over there, Hallie? While we slave away over here doing all the work?"

Hallie smiled mischievously, pointing a dripping spatula at Angie. "You have to come over here and help. You can make the first animal."

Angie pasted a smile on her face for Hallie, but the look she shot him over the girl's head made it clear she knew exactly what he was doing, and he would pay for it later.

He just smiled and stepped away from the stove, waving a hand toward the spot he'd vacated. "Your griddle awaits."

Her spine stiff as a poker, she came around the counter, flashing him a deadly glare when Hallie wasn't looking and refusing to actually step up to the stove.

Without an ounce of remorse he moved across the kitchen to the opposite counter, leaned against it, crossed his arms over his chest and settled in to enjoy the show.

Pointedly dismissing him, Angie took in the project before her as if trying to decide just how involved she was going to have to be. Could she maybe stay where she was and bark orders at Hallie? Or would she actually have to get in there and help, working side by side with the little girl?

Jason's lips twitched. Hot stove, six-year-old girl, *animal* pancakes. Barking orders was not going to be an option, and he saw the exact moment when Angie realized it, too.

Shooting him one final scowl, she drew a deep, fortifying breath and strode into action. "Okay, Hallie, I think you've just about beaten that batter to death. Let's give it a break, shall we, and test the griddle?"

Hallie glanced over her shoulder at her, her brows pulled low. "What are we testing it for?"

"To see how hot it is." Angie flipped the faucet on and briefly stuck two fingers under the fine stream of water.

"How hot does it have to be?"

"Hot enough to keep the animals from bleeding."

Hallie's eyes grew wide. "Bleeding?"

"Well, running is maybe a better word," Angie quickly reassured the little girl. "If the griddle isn't hot enough the batter runs and the shape of the animal is lost. So the griddle has to be hot."

"Okay. Are you gonna touch it? See if it's hot enough?" Worry creased Hallie's brow, making it obvious that she certainly didn't want to touch the griddle to test its readiness.

Jason smiled. Smart cookie.

But Angie's look was serious as she turned to the little girl. "Hallie, you know never to touch the stove or anything on it, right? It might be hot, and you'll get burned."

Hallie nodded. "Yeah, that's what Ms. Carmichael says, but how else are you going to test it?"

Angie held up her two fingers, dripping from their foray under the faucet. "Watch."

Angie stepped to the stove and flicked a couple of drops of water onto the griddle. "See how that water is just sitting there?"

Hallie nodded from her chair by the sink.

"That means it's not hot enough. When you put a drop of water on the griddle and it dances, it's ready." Angie walked back over to Hallie. "Here, hop down and we'll move you to the stove so you can watch. Then you can make the second pancake. Okay?"

Hallie nodded enthusiastically, jumping down from her chair. "Did you make animal pancakes when you were little?"

Angie nodded as she moved the chair to the stove. "Yep. It was a big tradition at our house on Saturday mornings. My mom and dad slept in so us kids had free rein over the kitchen. So we had contests to see who could make the best picture pancakes."

"Who won?"

Jason could see the grimace on Angie's profile as she turned to help Hallie back onto the chair. "My brother Ryan mostly. The little warmonger."

Hallie's brow crinkled, pulling her brows low as she turned around on the chair to face the stove. "What's that? A moremonger?"

Angie shook her head. "Never mind. Here, let's test the griddle again, shall we?"

Satisfaction ran through Jason as he watched the two of them. Although Angie had been stiff and uncertain when she'd first taken over, she was relaxing now. her motions returning to their usual graceful fluidness, her natural ability and joy with children coming to the fore.

Angie dropped another bead of water onto the grill, and this time it jumped and sizzled. "Perfect," she announced, grabbing the bowl of batter and a ladle from a nearby drawer. "Okay, the first thing you want to keep in mind is that things with big, fat proportions like elephants and teddy bears are easier to make than things with thin proportions like snakes and ballerinas."

Hallie nodded seriously as if she were receiving instructions on how to load a deadly weapon. "What are you going to make first?"

"I'm going to make a unicorn," Angie said, giving Hallie a broad smile and a conspiratorial wink.

Hallie's eyes lit up, and she rubbed her tiny hands together in glee. "Let's see."

Angie turned to the stove and went to work. "First I have to pour the eye and horn and mane separately and let them cook all by themselves for a minute, so they'll be a different color and stand out from the rest of the head. Then I'll pour the head and neck over them to tie them together and complete our unicorn."

Jason marveled at the precise instructions. She obviously had this down to a bloody art form.

Hallie apparently thought so, too. She watched Angie work as if she were watching Leonardo da Vinci create one of his masterpieces.

God, they were great together. And he was missing all the fun. "Hey, what about me? Do I get to make one?" he asked, snatching up his cane and heading to the stove.

Angie turned to him, spatula in hand. "After Hallie. But no guns," she warned.

He cocked a brow. "Guns?"

"Yes, guns. Or other weapons of mass destruction.

Ryan always turned his plate into a battlefield. Guns. Tanks. His specialty was a B-52 bomber dropping her load.''

Jason chuckled. ''I like it.''

She rolled her eyes. ''You would.'' Turning her back on him, she flipped her unicorn pancake onto a plate and then looked at him over her shoulder. ''Where's the syrup?''

''I don't have syrup, we'll have to use jam.''

Her eyes almost bugged out of her head, and she spun around to face him. ''Jam? On pancakes?''

''Yeah. Jam. Isn't that what Tom Sawyer ate on his pancakes?''

Angie wrinkled her nose in disgust and turned to Hallie. Leaning over, she whispered something in her ear.

Hallie giggled then copied Angie's expression, wrinkling her tiny, up-turned nose. They both turned to him. ''Eeeeew. Grr-oss. We want syrup,'' they chorused in perfect unison.

He laughed at the quickly choreographed performance, even if they were ganging up on him in his own kitchen. ''Sorry, gang, I don't have any.''

Angie huffed in exasperation. ''Come on, Jason, with your fancy pantries you have to have syrup here somewhere.''

''Why would I have syrup? I don't eat pancakes.''

Hallie's mouth fell open and she gave him a look of pure horror. ''You don't eat pancakes?''

''No, I don't, you little rugrat. Is that a crime?''

Angie turned to Hallie, her mouth twitching with suppressed humor, her brow lifted in conspiracy. Then once again they shifted their gazes to him simultaneously. ''Yes, it is,'' they chimed together.

He laughed again, shaking his head. ''Quit ganging up

on me.'' But he was loving every second of it. He'd never had a family, but he imagined it would be much like this. Lazy Saturday mornings, fancy breakfasts, easy teasing.

Angie laughed. ''What's wrong, soldier? Can't you take it?''

Hallie giggled.

Giggled. A light, tinkling sound of childhood and innocence and joy.

A sound he'd once hoped to hear on a regular basis. A bittersweet smile turned his lips. ''I can take it.''

But could he let it go? If his foray back into the real world didn't disintegrate before him he might be able to chase the silence and loneliness away during the days. But would the empty silence of these stone walls bring the madness back with the setting of the sun?

Rubbing her arms to ward off the chill, Angie stood in the cold, empty room, staring out the giant floor-to-ceiling window at the raging storm. The wind still howled like an angry wolf, its wild cry shrieking through the night as the snow swirled and raced frantically through the air.

It was late. She should be in bed, but she'd fled Dodge when Jason's voice, reading the adventures of Tom Sawyer, had started coming through the connecting door from Hallie's room as he'd tucked the little munchkin into bed. She wasn't up to listening to the time-honored tradition of reading to a child before lights out, a tradition she had once dreamed of sharing with her own children.

And being right across the hall from Jason wasn't a very wise place to be tonight, either. She wanted him. Wanted to walk across the hall into his bedroom and into his arms. She wanted him to hold her and love her and make her forget the loneliness swallowing her up. If only for tonight.

But going to him tonight wouldn't be any smarter than it would have been last night, so she'd bolted from her room and ended up here, in the second upstairs hall. She'd often wondered what was up the other staircase, and Jason had told her to feel free to explore anytime she wanted. Tonight was the perfect night for the little adventure.

The first two rooms she'd peeked into had appeared to be guest rooms, complete with queen-size beds and opulent decor, neither of which had beckoned her inside. But this barren room had, with its bare stone walls and shadowed corners and giant window. It was like standing inside an empty soul looking out on the world.

Which was exactly how she felt. Like her body was just a useless, empty shell where she stayed and stared out at the real world where other people lived and laughed and loved.

She sighed and leaned her forehead against the cool panes. She was tired of being alone. Tired of coming home to an empty apartment after spending days on the road. Tired of playing with her brothers' and sister's kids and pretending she was just fine without her own. Tired of going to bed alone night after night after night.

But being tired of it wouldn't change the circumstances that made her single lifestyle an unavoidable fact of life. It wouldn't make the loneliness go away, either—loneliness that had been chased away this morning for just a little bit while they'd all made animal pancakes together.

At least she and Hallie had made animal pancakes. Jason, the rat, had made a Fat Man, Little Boy set of atom bombs. She smiled to herself, drawing a nonsensical pattern on the condensation beading the window. Still, Fat Man and Little Boy bombs aside, for that one hour she'd felt like a normal person. Happy and complete.

But it was fluke. A single moment out of time. Soon

she'd go back to her world. Back to her empty apartment. Back to a job she liked mainly because it kept her too busy to think. Back to coloring with her brothers' and sister's kids.

Back to being just an observer. Pretending she was anything else was foolish. Which was why, after devouring more animal pancakes than could be good for anyone, she'd stayed in her room and worked on the Kent House piece for the rest of the day. And why perhaps, even knowing that Jason must have finished his story long ago, she was still here in this empty hall where Jason and temptation weren't at hand.

She shifted her gaze from the window to the only other entity that shared the room with her, the gargoyle hovering in the corner near the ceiling. His ugly face seemed to be chiding her for standing there, doing nothing more than brooding.

She smiled ruefully. The stone guardian was probably right. This damp, depressing room was doing nothing to improve her mood. And surely, in a house this unique, she could find something to occupy her time and imagination.

She pushed away from the window and left the empty room. Across the hall she turned the knob on the nearest door. Locked. She stepped back, curious. What was Jason keeping locked up?

A glint of metal caught her eye at the top left hand corner of the door. Looking up, she spied an old skeleton key.

Should she?

Curiosity got the best of her. She stretched up on her tiptoes, grabbed the key and fit it to the lock. Surely Jason wouldn't mind. He'd said she could explore. And if he hadn't wanted anyone in the room, surely he wouldn't have left the key hanging right next to the door.

An arsenal of weapons stared back at her from the opposite wall. No wonder Jason had the room locked. He'd once planned to have children here. He'd probably once entertained the children from Kent House here, too, and he wouldn't have wanted them to be able to get into this room. Hanging so far above the floor, the key would have been inaccessible to a child.

She stared at the array of weapons. Assault rifles, hunting rifles, hand guns and an amazing collection of wicked looking knives were mounted on a soft foam backboard for quick identification and easy access.

Surprised at the sheer volume of weapons in the arsenal, she strode over to the display. She'd seen many of the deadly little darlings before, most of them when she'd done her article on mercenaries. But there were a few she had never seen. She plucked a particularly nasty looking knife from its bracket, its serrated teeth glinting in the light. A shiver ran up her spine as she faced the harsh realities of Jason's previous life.

He'd fought so hard. These weapons were proof of the mortal danger he'd placed himself in time and time again in order to protect not only the country's freedom but the freedom of hundreds of individuals as well.

And in order to secure his future for the family and home he'd always desired. A dream he had yet to realize.

Bittersweet reality rushed through her. With his new-found decision to give the world another try, she felt sure it would be only a matter of time before he realized that dream. Some lucky woman would soon snatch him up and carry him away and give him exactly what he wanted—wedded bliss with a half dozen little Kent replicas to complete the picture.

A hollow, sinking feeling filled her stomach. The last thing she wanted to think about was Jason making babies with some other woman.

A sound behind her startled her, sending her heart into her throat. She spun around to find Jason walking into the room. "Lord, you scared me to death." She pressed her hand to her chest, trying to slow the pounding of her heart.

He raised a curious brow. "Who were you expecting?"

She smiled, embarrassment heating her cheeks. "I hate to admit it, but considering the contents of this room, anyone from Jack the Ripper to Count Dracula." She rotated her wrist, displaying every angle of the knife. "This sweetie alone evokes enough diabolical images to fill an acre with goose bumps."

He gave a noncommittal grunt and joined her at the display. Plucking the knife from her fingers, he returned it to its place on the wall. "It's effective, but you're right, it doesn't conjure up particularly reassuring images. And it definitely doesn't evoke the mood I was hoping for tonight."

She stilled, her heart rate picking up. She wanted to pretend she didn't know what kind of mood he'd been hoping for. But she knew. Lord, she knew. She'd spent all last night and all today trying not to think about his proposition. Trying not to think about how much she wanted his touch, how good his warmth would feel against the cold emptiness inside her.

And now, standing so close that his heat soaked into her skin, she held her breath and prayed that he wouldn't press the point.

He cocked his head to the side and watched her. "Are you going to leave me waiting again tonight, Angie?"

Closing her eyes, she shook her head. "Jason, don't."

"Why?"

Because I don't know if I'm strong enough to resist, and so much could go wrong if I say yes. She met his gaze, trying to make him understand. "Because, it's just…impossible."

"No it's not. In fact, it's the easiest thing in the world." He held his hand out to her, his expression gently reassuring. "Let me show you."

She stared at his hand, panic and need crashing inside her. She couldn't breathe, couldn't think with his heat soaking into her skin, those blue eyes looking into hers, reassuring her, promising her, entreating her.

She spun away from him, looking around desperately as if she would find the perfect answer to her dilemma written on the gray stones. But all she found was a collection of climbing equipment against one wall, a set of diving gear on another…and the open oak door.

Run.

The panicked voice echoed through her head. Run. Out the door, down the stairs and back up the stairs to her bedroom. She could be locked away safe and sound by the time Jason made it over there.

"I—" *Have to go.* But the words stuck in her throat, just as her feet stuck to the ground, refusing to run, refusing to move.

She heard him close the short distance between them, his cane tapping on the floor. He stopped directly behind her, his heat once again soaking into her back, his breath whispering through her hair. "You want this, Angie, as much as I do. Forget about what you think I need, and let us have tonight."

Her body tensed, and she clenched her fists at her sides, resisting the urge to reach back and touch him as she searched for any excuse to do the smart thing, the only sane thing.

But not the thing she wanted to do.

"What about Hallie?" she asked, a last ditch excuse to do the smart thing.

He gently placed his hand on her shoulder. "She's asleep. Has been for almost an hour."

Panic swamped her. She sent up her last flare. "What if she wakes up?"

"She's not going to wake up. She's a child. She still sleeps the sleep of the innocent. A nuclear blast wouldn't wake her." His reassurance was quiet, gently chiding.

She turned to face him, looking up into those intense sapphire eyes. "This is a big mistake."

He shook his head. "Never." And before she could take her next breath, his lips lowered to hers.

Soft.

Sweet.

Perfect.

Too perfect. She arched into him, needing more than his gentle touch. Needing him to chase away the emptiness that gnawed at her soul and threatened to swallow her whole. Needing to know that he wanted her as much as she wanted him.

As if he discerned her desperation he deepened the kiss and wrapped his arms tighter around her, pulling her closer, bringing her hard against the proof of his desire.

Yes. She put her arms around his neck, pulling him closer still, her tongue sparring desperately with his.

A purely male groan rumbled in his chest, but then he was pulling his lips from hers, his breathing hard and ragged. "Not here. God, not here. We're going to do this right, damn it. Not on the floor with death and destruction staring at us from the walls." He grasped her hand and pulled her from the room.

Chapter Twelve

Jason pulled Angie out of the arsenal and down the hall, ignoring her groan as he dragged her past the guest rooms—rooms that would serve their purpose just fine. Perfectly in fact. Except…he didn't want her in those rooms. He wanted her in *his* room. Like a caveman dragging his woman off to *his* cave, no other cave would do.

Arrogant and juvenile, but man had been carrying his woman back to his abode for millennia. There had to be something to it. And tonight was important. He might have only this one chance to prove that he had more to offer her than a shattered knee and a scarred face.

Not that he was asking for happily ever after. He had never believed in fairy tales. In real life Beauty never settled down with the Beast. But he was hoping that by the end of the night, the knee and face wouldn't be the first thing that came to mind when she thought of him.

And he wanted to undo some of the damage worm

Steven had done. By morning he wanted her to know she was the most precious thing on earth. He wanted to praise her with his lips and worship her with his hands until she understood just how special she was.

His heart pounding in his chest, blood rushing into his ears, he finally pulled her into his room. "This is where I want you." He pulled her into his arms and settled his lips once more on hers.

She wrapped her arms around him eagerly, pulling him closer, straining against him as if she couldn't get close enough.

He knew exactly where she was coming from. He'd seen the sadness and loneliness in her eyes when he'd gone into the armory. He knew that's why she was in his arms now. Because she couldn't stand the loneliness one more second. A feeling he understood intimately.

He hugged her tighter, kissed her deeper, answering her desperate need while trying to keep his own from spiraling out of control. His hands shook as he ran them down her back, taking in her soft, feminine curves, the delicate turn of her back, the inviting roundness of her hips. Heaven on earth. He spread his legs wide and pulled her closer, hard up against his arousal.

She moaned softly and dropped her hands to his hips, pulling him closer still, adjusting her hips to give them both the pleasure they sought.

Need rushed through his veins like fire through a wind tunnel. He wanted to touch her. Needed to touch her. Not her sweater. Not the rough texture of her jeans. Her. He slipped his hands under her sweater, his fingers gliding over her waist.

Oh, man. She was so soft and so tiny and so damned…perfect.

A hard shudder ran through him as he greedily explored

the warm expanse of skin, savoring the delicate feel of her, the pure feminine shape of her. He moved his hands over the easy curve of her waist, the fragile expanse of her rib cage and up to the gentle swell of her breast. A silent groan echoed through his head.

More material.

This, soft and slippery, but still, a damned poor second to the warm satin of her skin. His fingers itched to touch the abundant flesh of her breasts. His palms ached to cup their heavy fullness. He pulled his lips from hers, gasping for air. "The clothes have to go, Angie. I want to feel you. Just you."

"Yes." Her fingers flew to his shirt and she started popping buttons free as she rained quick, hungry kisses over his face and down his neck. "Hurry. I need you."

The statement slammed through him like a megadose of the strongest aphrodisiac. He needed her, too. He slipped his hands out of her sweater and grabbed the bottom to pull it over her head.

Suddenly she panicked, pushing his hands away. "Wait, wait—" She pulled away from him, her plea as desperate as it was breathless. "The lights. Turn off the lights first."

"I want to see you." His voice was rough with desire.

She shook her head, closing her eyes, panic marring the desire on her face. "Please, Jason."

Of course, his scars. Something twisted in his gut, but he ignored it. By the end of this night he hoped to convince her, and himself perhaps, that the scars weren't who he was. But this wasn't the end of the night, and right now, she obviously wasn't up to facing the not-so-pleasant parts of him.

He refused to let it bother him. The scars *were* bad. Hell, there were mornings when *he* couldn't face them.

He tipped his head toward the switch. "Okay. Turn them off."

Relief flashed in her eyes and then she raced for the switch by the door. The room was plunged into darkness, and then she was in front of him again, all warm and wiggly and shivering with need.

He closed his hands over her hips, pulling her to him, glad she was in this room with him at all. Denim and soft cotton bunched beneath his fingers. "There are still too many clothes here." This time when he grabbed hold of her sweater she didn't stop him.

He effortlessly pulled the soft cotton up and over her head, tossing it into the dark. The blood pounded faster in his veins as the scent of jasmine stirred in the air.

Her fingers made quick work of the rest of his buttons, and then she whipped his shirt down his shoulders, off his wrists and into the darkness with hers.

He pulled her into his arms with a sigh of pure, male gratification as skin stroked against skin.

Just one little barrier still in the way. With shaky hands he reached behind her, unclasped the bit of satin and lace still blocking his touch and slid it down her arms. And then there was nothing but burning heat and the fine sheen of sweat between them.

His groin pounded harder, anticipation slicing through him as he slid his hands up her rib cage. Up…up…

Paradise.

She was full and heavy and…magnificent. His fingers kneaded the warm, inviting flesh, heat pouring through him, need slicing him to the bone.

Inhaling on a sharp breath, she leaned into his hands, her hips bumping against his, her fingers digging into his shoulders. The sound of her pleasure threatened to send his own desire over the edge, his erection flexing painfully behind his fly. But he wouldn't be rushed, even by his own need. Proper worship took time. Reveling in the feel of her breasts, he took her nipples between thumb and finger and gently squeezed.

A soft groan slipped from her lips. Clinging to his shoulders, she leaned forward and nipped at his lower lip. "More," she pleaded, her voice tight with passion.

Oh, yeah. He teased her nipples again, gently rotating them between his fingers.

She shuddered against him, making tiny mewing sounds in her throat.

He closed his lips over hers, thrusting his tongue deep, letting her know exactly where they were headed. Time to get rid of the rest of the barriers. Shaking more than he had the first time he'd disarmed an antipersonnel land mine, he dropped his hands to the waistband of her jeans, popped the snap open and pushed her jeans and panties from her hips.

They landed on the floor with a soft sigh. He pulled his lips from hers. "Step out of them."

"Hold on. My shoes." She held onto his shoulders for balance as she levered off first one shoe and then the other.

When he heard the second shoe come free he guided her forward a step, his fingers sinking into the soft flesh of her hips. Soft, naked, female hips. Oh, *man.*

Before he had time to shuck his own pants, she was pressing herself against him again, hotly, urgently, as if the few seconds she hadn't been snuggled up against him had been far too long.

It had felt like a lifetime to him, too. He pulled her close, reclaiming her lips and savoring the feel of her cute little naked butt snuggled into his greedy palms.

She quivered in his arms, moaning softly. And then she

was sliding one of her knees up his leg, bringing her hips closer to his, opening herself to him.

His fingers dug into her hips, his manhood flexing against her. His damned chinos were the only thing keeping him from heaven, but he couldn't do anything about them now. Not with her snuggled up closer than skin and the very essence of her femininity within reach. He pulled her knee higher, hooking it over his hip. And then he slid his hand down her leg toward her thigh. Down and around and in toward the very center of her.

His fingertips grazed her moist heat, testing, teasing.

She moaned a little louder, her hips automatically rocking forward, her tongue sparring more urgently with his.

Slowly, deliberately, he slipped a finger inside.

Her knees collapsed, sending her down.

Moving one hand behind her back, he kept his lips on hers as he followed her down, gentling her fall and laying her carefully beneath him. She wrapped her knees around him, cradling his hips with hers as they settled on the floor.

His hips thrust against hers, his libido getting way ahead of the game. If he didn't slow things down, the only thing she would remember in the morning was how fast he was. And taking her on the floor was hardly going to make her feel special. Also, there was one other matter they had to deal with.

He pulled his lips from hers, his breathing hard and fast. "Angie, wait. I've got protection, but it's in the nightstand. Let me get it. Besides, I didn't drag you all the way over here to make love to you on the floor."

Her hands tightened on his shoulders and she pulled him back as if her very life depended on his presence. "Forget the protection. I've got it covered. And forget the bed, too. I don't need it. I need you, Jason. *Now.* Don't leave me alone. Even for a second.''

He gritted his teeth against the blood pounding in his groin. He wanted her to feel cherished, not ravished. ''But—''

She shook her head frantically, her hair snapping against his wrists. *''Jason.''* The word was a strangled plea, an impatient demand.

Screw it. He'd worship her later. Right now she seemed to know exactly what she needed.

And so did he. He unfastened his waistband, unzipped his pants, shoved them to his knees. And pushed inside her.

Stars exploded in his head. Hot. Wet. Tight. He gritted his teeth to keep from losing it right there. He didn't want to hurt her and he suspected it had been a long while since she'd been with a man. So he clenched his fists and remained as still as nature would allow while he gave her time to adjust to his invasion.

A gesture she didn't seem to appreciate at all. Whimpering beneath him, she raised her hips to his and clawed at his back. ''Don't hold back on me now, Jason. Please.''

A plea he couldn't ignore. He gave his passion free rein, plunging deep, taking everything that she would give, giving everything that he had. Taking and giving until they were no longer separate entities, but two people connected in the most intimate dance as they nurtured and soothed and pushed each other to dizzying heights…and shattering release.

He collapsed on top of her, leaning on his elbows to keep from crushing her. When he finally had enough breath to talk, he asked, ''Better?''

She nodded, her head rubbing against his shoulder.

''Good.'' He gathered her closer, savoring the feel of

her skin against his, the scent of sweet jasmine tickling his senses, her warmth wrapped around him.

Slowly, their breathing evened out. A small cramp seized his calf. Trying to ease it, he shifted on his elbows, the rough nap of the carpet biting into his skin.

The floor. He chuckled into the darkness. Some Romeo he was.

She wiggled beneath him. "What are you laughing at?"

"I dragged you all the way over here because I wanted to do this right." He shook his head in disbelief. "And we ended up on the floor."

She laughed, the sound husky and well sated. "Trust me, you did it right."

A smile of pure satisfaction turned his lips. "Yeah?"

She laughed again, thrusting her hips up, pushing him deeper. "Yeah."

Fresh blood surged to his manhood. "Oh, lady, unless you're serious, don't start that."

She kissed his jaw, rocking against him once more. "I'm serious, soldier."

Thank the stars. He kissed her quick, hard and deep, then rolled away before her entreaty got any more persuasive. "Hold that thought, we're changing our venue. This time we're doing it right. Slow, easy...and in bed." Before she could protest he pushed to his feet.

Angie groaned from the floor. "I don't think I can move."

He chuckled as he bent over and felt for her hand in the dark. Once he located it, he pulled her to her feet. "Come on, you'll like the bed better. I promise."

As he led her to the bed, his gait uneven and awkward without the use of his cane, he was grateful for the darkness.

She reached for him as soon as they rolled into the thick folds of his down comforter, her grasp almost as frantic as it had been earlier.

He gently knocked her hands aside. "Nope. My way now. Slow. And easy. And sweet." He slid up next to her, his body running down the length of hers as he propped himself up on one elbow.

Beside him she laughed, soft and slightly indignant. "You had complaints about my way?"

He chuckled with her, his body leaping to life at the mere thought of her energetic ways. "No, it was great. It's just my turn now."

She wiggled, her body stroking impatiently against his. "Jason," she all but whined.

He laughed quietly, finding her collarbone in the dark and lightly trailing his fingertips down between her breasts to the delicate indentation of her navel, where he made slow, lazy circles. "No whining. We'll get there. But first, I want you to know how beautiful you are." He leaned down and kissed her softly at the temple. "How wonderful you are." His lips found her nose. "How absolutely, positively, undeniably exquisite you are."

"Oh." The sigh was whisper thin as she stretched sensuously beside him. "By all means, let's do it your way."

"Smart lady." He dropped light, butterfly kisses on her eyelids. "You have the most beautiful eyes. Like harvest wheat with a sprinkling of emeralds hanging from their tassels."

She sighed softly and kissed his chin again. "Jason Kent, you're a romantic."

He gave his head a wry shake. "I never have been before, but tonight, for you, I want to be," he admitted, feeling a bit out of his element, hoping he wouldn't make a complete ass of himself. "I'll try to avoid comparing you to something really odious, but, be warned, anything could happen.'' Particularly since the most active part of his body right now *wasn't* his brain.

She smiled against the soft underside of his chin. ''Women like bumbling Cyranos—it tells us the line hasn't been used on a hundred women before us.''

''Yeah?''

Her lips moved against his throat again. ''Yeah. Tell me more,'' she whispered into the dark.

He dropped a soft, soulful kiss on her lips. He compared her to the sweetest of fruits, the rarest of jewels, the loveliest of flowers. He kissed her and tasted her and explored her. He touched her and teased her and tantalized her until she begged for mercy.

And then he joined his body to hers, sending them both soaring up and up...and over.

''Jason,'' she whispered in his ear as she shuddered hard beneath him.

He held her beneath him, breathing in her scent, savoring the feel of her soft body against his. Heaven on earth.

Eventually, their hearts slowed their crazy pounding and their bodies cooled. When he felt her shiver beneath him, he rolled off and pulled her close. Grabbing the covers, he wrapped them in soft down to protect them from the room's chill.

She moved against him, laying her head on his shoulder and draping her naked little body over the right half of his.

He ran his hand over her arm, savoring the intimacy. She felt soft and warm and boneless lying against him.

She rubbed her cheek against his chest. ''I like this. Just lying in your arms.''

He pulled her closer, giving her a gentle hug. "I like you here."

"Can I stay the night?"

You can stay forever. "Yes."

"I need to get up before Hallie does. I don't want her finding us together."

Unfortunately, she was right, that wouldn't be good. "I'll wake you at sunrise."

Suddenly she stiffened in his arms, not a lot, but enough for him to notice. "I should go before it gets light."

He went still. She'd begged for his touch. Cried out his name as she'd crested the waves of passion. But she still couldn't face him in the light.

He closed his eyes against the despair pounding at his heart. He was what he was. He couldn't go back and avoid the blast that had taken out his knee. He couldn't go back and stay the hand of the man who'd slashed his face. This is what he had. And if Angie couldn't face it...

He rubbed her arm again as if he could soothe the pain in his own heart with the comforting gesture. "Go to sleep. I'll wake you before dawn."

Chapter Thirteen

Angie stared at her reflection in the bathroom mirror and pulled the brush through her hair for the thousandth time, bees buzzing in her veins, a herd of elephants tromping over her nerves. Last night had been…incredible. More than incredible. No words were strong enough, beautiful enough to describe what Jason had done to her last night. For a few wonderful hours he'd made her feel…

Cherished.

She couldn't ever remember feeling as if she were the most important person in the world. Ever. But last night, Jason had made her feel that way.

So why wasn't she with him now?

She knew why. And it had nothing to do with the fact that leaving his arms this morning had been the hardest thing she'd ever done. Or that every minute she spent with him from now on would only make it harder to leave him when the plows finally made it up this road.

No, she'd already resigned herself to that pain. If Jason wanted her back in his bed, she'd be there. She couldn't turn her back on something as wonderful as what they'd shared last night.

She hadn't gone looking for Jason for one reason and one reason only. Morning-after jitters. She'd acted like a crazed nymphomaniac last night. In the dark that had seemed just fine, but looking Jason in the eye in the light of day? Lordy, heat bloomed on her cheeks just thinking about it.

But she couldn't put off facing him any longer. She'd finished putting all her notes into prose about half an hour ago. Now, to finish the article, she needed more details.

Setting her brush down, she snatched up her pen and notebook from where she'd set them on the top of the commode and rushed from the bathroom before she chickened out and went back to her room. Jogging down the stairs, she glanced across the foyer at the study. Although the doors were closed, she could hear the sound of cartoons emanating from the room. Hallie was watching TV. Alone, or with Jason?

Hopefully alone. A lot of the questions she had to ask about Hallie and Kent House would best be asked without the little girl's presence. Also, if Hallie were with them they'd have to pretend nothing had happened last night. And she didn't want to pretend right now.

She glanced at the office door. Light flickered in the dark space between the door and floor. Yes. It looked like he was working. Taking a deep breath, she strode to the office door, knocked once and pushed her way in.

* * *

At the sound of the knock Jason double-clicked the image of the property he was interested in and then swiveled in his chair to face the door.

Angie. Looking shy and flushed and a little bit breathless.

Relief poured through him. He'd been down here all day wondering if she was ever going to seek him out. Wondering if she was staying away because she was back into her isolationist mode, or if she was staying away because she regretted going to bed with him.

Useless thoughts, all of them. Angie wasn't ever going to see him as anything more than the beast. If he was smart he'd walk away from what they'd shared last night, count his blessings and get on with his life.

But no matter how many times he'd told himself during the night to back off, to send her on her way before morning light and stay the hell away from her from then on, he couldn't convince himself to do it. Even now he tried to squelch the pleasure swelling in his chest at the mere sight of her, the blood stirring in his veins. But it was futile. He wanted her—however much she was willing to give. "I'm glad you finally came down. I missed you this morning."

The color on her cheeks darkened, the shy smile twitched. "I was embarrassed. I think I might have been a little exuberant last night."

He met her gaze straight on, letting her see just how much he'd enjoyed last night. "You didn't embarrass me."

Her smile broadened. "Good. Does that mean I might be able to talk you into a good-morning kiss, even though it's afternoon? I've been thinking about it all day."

So had he. He crooked his finger at her.

She strode over to him, those bee-stung lips smiling seductively as she closed the distance between them. Stepping to the side of his chair she leaned down and pressed her lips to his.

Soft and sweet. But it didn't stay that way for long. Electricity crackled between them, igniting their senses and kicking up the heat in a damned short minute. He ran his hand through her hair, capturing her head. Pulling her closer, he nudged at her lips with his tongue.

She opened to him immediately, taking his tongue inside, matching his rhythm with a feminine dance of her own.

Fire charged through his veins, white-hot and lightning quick. Last night had obviously done more to feed the fire than quench it. With a frustrated groan he gently pulled his lips from her and pushed her back a step. ''We've got to stop this right now, or you're going to find yourself in my lap.'' He locked his gaze with hers. ''Sans jeans.''

Heat burned in her eyes. Leaning back into him, she tried to recapture his lips with hers. ''Sounds good to me.''

He snatched a quick kiss. ''Me, too. But we can't.'' He stole another taste. ''Hallie.''

She straightened as if she'd been jabbed with a bayonet, her breathing as erratic as his. ''You're right.'' Stepping away from him, she tugged at her sweater and ran a quick hand through her hair, but the look she gave him was one of pure misery.

He reached out and touched her hand. ''Don't worry, we'll make up for it tonight.''

She drew in a slow, shaky breath. ''I'm going to hold you to that, soldier.''

And more fool he, he would let her, knowing full well she'd never accept more from him than temporary solace.

He tipped his head toward the paper and pen in her hand. "Did you come down here for more than a kiss?"

She chuckled softly. "I need more information on Hallie for the story. Deadline's tomorrow, so I need to finish up today."

"You going to call it in, or fax it?"

Her eyes lit up. "You have a fax?"

He nodded toward a cabinet set underneath his counter. "In there."

She did a little dance. "Yes. I hate calling these things in." She moved to the bank of computers and pulled herself up onto the curved counter. Once she was comfortable, her feet swinging a good foot off the floor, she reclaimed her writer's tools.

Jason crossed his ankle over his knee, getting comfortable. "What do you need to know?"

"Since Hallie's heart is going to be one of the biggest concerns for prospective parents, I need details about her problem. The medical term for it and a general rundown of what it is. How it affects her. What treatments she's undergone in the past. Prognosis for the future. That kind of thing."

"Hallie was born with a congenital heart defect called Tetralogy of Fallot. Doctors and nurses call these kids blue babies because their hearts don't provide the children with enough oxygen. Hence, they're born cyanotic, with a blue tint to their skin."

She scribbled industriously, her brows pulled down in concern. "Why aren't they getting enough oxygen? Is the heart too small? Inoperative? What?"

"It's complicated. But Hallie's doctor described it to me this way. At one place there's a hole in the heart that doesn't belong, and in another an obstruction. As a result, the blood doesn't circulate correctly and the baby ends up without enough oxygen.''

She nodded, looking up from her note pad. ''How do they fix it? They do fix it, don't they? Hallie's small, but she seems pretty healthy to me, and she said they fixed her heart.''

''They did fix it—with surgery, and she is healthy. Now. TOF is generally corrected with two surgeries. The first is done as soon after birth as possible to increase blood flow to the lungs; and the second, when the child is between three to five to correct the defect itself. Generally speaking, the child has few to no problems once the second surgery is complete.''

She grimaced as his words trailed off. ''But there are no guarantees.''

He tipped his head in agreement.

''That's why she hasn't been adopted, isn't it? People are afraid there'll be future problems.'' Sadness echoed in her voice, and her eyes took on a suspicious sheen.

''Yes.''

She drew in a deep breath and blew it out through puffed cheeks. ''I have got to write a great article here, Jason. I have to convince one wonderful, loving set of parents that Hallie is worth the risk.''

This from a woman who was so afraid of personal involvement that she hadn't dated in the last five years, who was so afraid of getting personally attached to Hallie that she'd avoided the kid like she had the plague. A ghost of a smile pulled at his lips. ''Good idea. Are *you* going to read it when you're done?''

Her eyes narrowed to hazel bands. ''Are you implying something here?''

"Just that you want someone else to take this big risk, and you're afraid to be in the same room with her."

Pain flashed in her eyes. "It's not the same."

"Isn't it?"

"No. Couples are turning her down because they're afraid she won't fulfill their dreams. I'm staying away because I can't fulfill hers."

There it was again, that martyr's theme that kept cropping up. Not for the first time in the last twelve hours he wondered which issues were keeping them apart the most—his infirmities or her fears. "I don't suppose you'd like to share the details behind that skewed train of thought, would you?"

Her lips compressed. "No."

"I didn't think so. But just for the record. Hallie wants to see you. She asked about you at breakfast and again at lunch."

Angie dropped her head and rubbed her eyes with her fingers. "Tell her I'm busy writing the article."

"I'm not going to lie for you."

She looked up at him, her expression bleak but resigned. "Fine. If she comes looking for me, I'll make my own excuses."

He was sure she would. She'd gotten pretty good at hiding behind the walls she'd put up around herself. He tipped his head toward the notebook in her lap. "Where were we?"

She looked back at her notes. "I think I have enough on the heart. Now I need to know how she ended up in a group home. What happened to her parents?"

"Her parents were killed in a boating accident when she was two. At that point she was shuffled into the state system where she stayed until she was four, which was when one of my people came across her file and brought it to my attention.

"Ms. O'Niel pointed out that the state had been plowing through red tape for almost a year trying to get Hallie's second surgery done. And it looked like it would be another year before everything was finalized. We didn't think Hallie should wait that long. According to the records, she wasn't in imminent danger, but she was getting weaker. To make a long story short, we brought her to Kent House, had the surgery done immediately and settled her in."

She shook her head sadly. "A boating accident and a state system that worries more about paperwork than little children. Lord, having been born with a defective heart wasn't enough, she needed a little more misery piled on top?"

He shrugged, not dismissively, but because he knew life was more often cruel than not. "She's a tough kid. She'll make it. At Kent House, we'll see that she makes it."

"How is she doing at Kent House? Does she like it?"

"She likes it as well as any kid can like institutional living. It's not a home. It's as good or better than a lot of foster homes, but it's not a real home. It never will be."

"How about behavioral problems? These first six years of her life haven't been easy. How is she holding up?"

He gave her a wry smile. "Just in case it escaped your notice, when things get to be too much for her, she runs away."

Her lips quirked into a smile. "Yes, she does, doesn't she?"

He ran a worried hand down his face. "In the past it didn't worry me so much. You know, little kids get mad or upset and run away, usually no farther than the backyard. Then, when they get hungry, they come back. And that had been Hallie's pattern until now.'' He shook his head, a chill running down his spine as he pictured Hallie out in the storm on her sled, a lot farther than the orchard that made up Kent House's backyard. ''But this time the outcome could have been deadly.''

Angie's expression mirrored his own concern. ''It could have been, but it wasn't.'' Her expression softened, mischief sneaking into her amber eyes. ''And look at all the great stories she'll have to tell the kids when she goes back. Great tales of spooky old haunted houses—'' She circled her finger, indicating the house at large.

''Goblins and ghouls.'' She pointed to the gargoyle sitting in the top right hand corner of the room. ''And a kindly old caretaker who feeds lost children soup and animal pancakes until they're coming out their ears.'' She pointed her finger at him with a cheeky grin.

He cocked a challenging brow. ''Old?''

She laughed softly, seductively. ''Well, maybe not *too* old.''

He snorted and pointedly dropped his gaze to the notebook in her hand. ''Don't you have work to do?''

Laughing easily, she jumped from the counter and walked toward him, her hips swaying softly from side to side. ''Yeah, I do. And if I'm going to have this done by tomorrow I do need to get on it.'' She stopped at his chair, her expression turning hesitant, vulnerable. ''Are you sure you want me to come tonight?''

He should tell her no. Waking her up before dawn and sending her on her way had been a sharp reminder that she wasn't going to see beyond his flaws. And seeing how she distanced herself from Hallie told him that she wasn't going to let anyone beyond the walls she'd built around herself, either. When those plows came up this road, she would be gone. Well and truly gone.

But it didn't matter. He couldn't make it matter. When she laughed as she had only moments before, with fun and mischief shining in her eyes, he wanted her. Standing beside him now, looking heart-stoppingly vulnerable, he wanted her. So badly he ached.

He reached out and took her hand. Raising it to his lips, he dropped a kiss on the back of her knuckles. "I want you to come."

Crash!

The sound brought Angie out of a deep, peaceful sleep. After Jason had spent the night testing her limits, she wasn't sure she'd ever be able to move again. She definitely wasn't sure the sound was worth leaving the warm cocoon of Jason's bed.

Unfortunately, Jason wasn't of the same opinion. He quickly shifted her off his shoulder and snapped up, wide awake and battle ready. Three years of retirement obviously hadn't dulled his field readiness.

She groaned into the dark and managed to pry one eye open. "What is it?"

"I don't know." He pulled the chain on the lamp next to the bed. Soft light filled the room and he glanced quickly around, his head coming to an abrupt halt as he looked toward the curtained window. "What the—"

Angie managed to lever herself up on an elbow so she could look where Jason was staring. A cinder block-sized piece of stone lay between the bed and the heavy brocade curtains covering the window. "Good Lord, Jason. Your mansion is falling down around our ears."

They both glanced up at the ceiling, she fully expecting

to see other pieces of stone falling from their moorings. But not only was nothing else falling, she couldn't even see where the present stone had fallen from. The arched ceiling looked completely intact.

They glanced at each other.

"Okay, that's enough of a mystery to get me out of bed." She reluctantly pushed herself up and grabbed Jason's robe from its heap on top of the covers. Pulling it on, she rolled out of bed, moved around the foot of it and stepped cautiously over to the stone. She nudged it with her foot. Its rough sides glinted gray in the light. "Definitely part of the castle."

They both peered at the ceiling again.

"Okay, it's dark," she admitted. "Maybe we're just not seeing the hole it fell from."

"Maybe." Jason snatched his pants from the floor and started pulling them on.

She knelt beside the stone, taking a closer look. The side facing up was jagged, as if it had broken off of a bigger piece. Reaching forward, she turned the heavy stone over. A ghoulish, macabre face stared back at her.

She shrieked at the threatening facade, then giggled as she realized what she was looking at. "You little beast, you got me." She looked over her shoulder at Jason and pointed toward the top right-hand corner of the room. "One of your guardians has abandoned his watchtower."

Dressed in only his pants, his broad, muscled shoulders catching the lamp's light, he looked up at the corner and then back to the gargoyle. "I'll be damned."

She stared down at the ghoul. He was busily chomping on some poor interloper's leg. Funny, when he'd been up in the corner his expression had always seemed fierce. But now, up close, he just looked…worried.

Thump.

A shot of adrenaline slammed through her veins, and she snapped her head around to look at Jason. "Please tell me I was kidding earlier when I referred to this place as a haunted house. You *don't* have ghosts, do you?"

He shook his head, his expression intent as he strained his ears listening for the next sound.

She lowered her voice to a whisper, her heart tripping against her ribs. "That was the front door, wasn't it?"

His brows snapped together like warring thunderclouds. "Hallie."

Fear slammed through her. "Running away?"

He nodded as he grabbed his shirt from the floor and started pulling it on. "Check her room."

She shot to her feet and raced out of the room, across the hall, and slammed through the door to the pink palace. The room wasn't any brighter than Jason's, but it was light enough to see that Hallie's bed was empty.

She spun back toward Jason. "She's gone."

Anticipating the worst, Jason was already jerking on his shoes. "Damn it."

She turned back to stare out Hallie's window. The winds were supposed to die down tonight. But they hadn't. Snow still plummeted through the air at an alarming rate. If Hallie got lost in that, she was in big trouble.

She pushed away from Hallie's door. "I'm going after her." Turning toward the staircase, she raced down the hall, her bare feet slapping frantically on the stone floor.

"Put on some shoes," Jason hollered after her. "You'll freeze out there."

"No time," she hollered back. "I've got to catch her before she gets away from the yard lights. It's too dark to find her in the forest. Come as soon as you can.'' She inwardly winced as she realized the blow those words would deliver to Jason's pride.

He was used to being the man who stepped in and saved the day. He would hate being left behind while she ran after Hallie, hate knowing the little munchkin might be in danger and he couldn't help. But there wasn't anything she could do about it now.

Jason had a tough enough time getting around when the footing was even; he'd never be able to chase Hallie in the snow. If anyone was going to catch the little runaway it would have to be her.

She leapt down the staircase two stairs at a time. Nearing the bottom, she vaulted over the last four stairs all together. She raced across the foyer and slammed out the door.

She saw Hallie the second she hit the porch. The little girl hadn't tried to be a bit coy as she made her escape. She'd simply walked out the door and headed straight across the open field toward the forest and the hill she'd come crashing down days ago. And the deep snow was keeping her progress slow. Thank God.

"Hallie, wait!" she hollered above the howling winds, leaping off the porch into the savage gale and freezing landscape.

Hallie stopped in her tracks and glanced over her shoulder. But seeing Angie didn't get her to head back to the house. She turned around and headed once again for the forest, doubling her speed.

Angie ran faster, the robe flying open and exposing her bare legs to the raw elements, her bare feet plunging through the icy snow. "Hallie, wait for me."

But the little girl just ran faster, the hood of her coat

bobbing against her back, her tiny body practically being swallowed up by the drifts as she got closer and closer to the dark forest.

Thankfully, Hallie's legs weren't much longer than a big grasshopper's. Angie was catching up fast. The little runaway was only thirty feet ahead of her now. Thirty feet. Twenty feet. Ten feet. Two. Angie reached out and grabbed the bright blue bouncing hood. "Gotcha."

Hallie rounded on her like a little wildcat, her tiny fist crashing into Angie's arm. "Let me go!"

"Ouch." The unexpected attack knocked Angie's hold loose, but before Hallie could break away, Angie regrouped and scooped the child into her arms.

The little bundle of down and snow-covered curls thrashed in her arms, twisting her agile little body this way and that in an attempt to get away.

"Damn it, Hallie, quit fighting me. I don't have any shoes on, and I'm freezing to death."

"Good," Hallie yelled, twisting her body viciously. "I *want* you to freeze to death."

Angie gritted her teeth and grabbed hold of her temper as she struggled through the snow toward the house, holding on to the fighting child with all her strength. "Well, thank you very much. I love you, too."

Hallie's tiny heel connected to her shin. "No you don't, you hate me."

Angie froze in her tracks, the wind biting through her skin, the icy snow slicing into her feet. "What?"

"You hate me." The words were angry and tearful and sounded as if they'd been torn from the little girl's heart.

Jason's words from earlier this afternoon echoed through Angie's head. *Hallie wants to see you. She asked about you at breakfast and again at lunch.*

And then her own words whispered guiltily through her head. *Tell her I have work to do.*

A giant lump formed in her throat and she had to force herself to talk through it. "No I don't, Hallie. I don't."

"Yes you do." She tried again to twist free. "That's why you won't come downstairs and be with Jason and me. Because you can't stand to be around me. No one can stand to be around me. That's why I'll never be adopted."

Angie's heart twisted as she imagined the pain the little girl was feeling. Pain that she had contributed to. Somehow she had to make Hallie see that it wasn't true, but first she had to get them back into the house before they froze to death. Her feet were going numb and her fingers weren't far behind.

Ignoring Hallie's protests, she tightened her grip and headed back to the mansion. Looking through the driving snow to make sure she was headed in the right direction, she found Jason standing on the porch, waiting.

She briefly closed her eyes against the frustration she knew he was feeling, standing there on the porch doing nothing but watching her haul Hallie through the blowing snow.

Lord, this night was turning into a nightmare.

As she made her way onto the porch she cast Jason an apologetic look. "Sorry, I know you don't want to be standing here."

"Forget it. The important thing is you got her."

The anger and impatience in his voice stung her, even though she knew it was directed at himself and not at her.

He opened the door for her so she could drag the kicking and squirming child into the warm foyer.

As soon as she was inside and she heard Jason close the door behind her, she let the angry little girl go.

Hallie immediately bolted. Where she was going seemed uncertain. Her only goal seemed to be getting away.

"Stop right there, young lady." The sharp command came from Jason. "You and I are going to have a little chat."

To Angie's surprise, Hallie stopped dead in her tracks. Spinning back toward them, she glared at Jason with tears pouring down her face. "What?"

"Where did you think you were going in this storm?"

"Away from here. Away from her," Hallie spat, pointing an angry, mittened hand at Angie. "She hates me."

Jason cast Angie a quick glance—one that seemed to hold both disappointment that she'd let Hallie down and empathy with how badly he knew she felt now—before refocusing on Hallie. "Angie does not hate you, and running away wouldn't fix it if she did. Remember what we talked about this fall in the orchard? About how running away doesn't help? When you're feeling bad you go to someone and talk to them. Remember?"

Those perfect little Cupid's lips pursed angrily. "I like to be alone."

"Yeah, well, in a storm like this you could be alone forever."

Angie's stomach clenched at the words. Had that gargoyle not fallen from the ceiling and awakened them, they would never have heard the front door shut behind Hallie. They wouldn't have known she had fled into the night until it was far too late.

And it would have been all her fault. Pain slashed at her heart and tears stung her eyes. She wanted to run to

Hallie and pull her into her arms, reassuring herself that the little munchkin was all right. But she had a feeling Jason wouldn't appreciate the interference, so she stayed still, guilt pounding at her heart.

Hallie wasn't nearly so affected by Jason's warning. She stood with her legs spread wide, her little arms crossed over her chest and a mutinous expression that clearly said she didn't care.

Jason cocked a knowing brow at the stubborn pose. "I think we'll finish this discussion in the morning. After you've had time to form your apology."

Hallie's eyes opened wide. "Apology?"

"Absolutely. You get me out of my bed in the middle of the night, scare me to death and drag me out into a hellacious storm. I want an apology. I imagine Angie wants one, too."

No, Angie wanted to scream, but when she stepped forward with the word forming on her lips Jason shot her a sharp, silencing glance, making it clear that he was handling this problem.

She rocked back on her heels, feeling worse and worse with each passing second.

"Fine," Hallie spat in petulant disgust.

"Fine," Jason echoed. "Now take your coat and boots off and go on up to your room."

With jerky, angry movements, tears still rolling down her cheeks, Hallie pulled off her coat and boots, threw them in a pile by the coat rack, stomped across the foyer and up the stairs and disappeared down the hall.

The knot in Angie's stomach tightened. Hallie's anger was just show. It was her tears that told the real story. And Angie was responsible for every one of those tears.

As soon as Hallie was out of earshot, she rounded on

Jason. "Why were you so hard on her? It wasn't her fault."

Despite her sharp tone, his expression remained calm, cool. "Of course it's her fault. She's the one who ran away."

"Because I made her feel bad."

"Yes, you did." The words held no accusation, but he didn't try to soften them. "But it's a hard world out there. You won't be the last person to make her feel bad. She needs to learn to deal with her problems in a different way, taking responsibility for her actions is a place to start."

She paced away from him. He was right. Hallie needed to stop running away. But it didn't change the fact that the little girl had run tonight because Angie had hurt her. She turned back to him, quickly wiping at the tears threatening to spill over. "I really screwed up, didn't I?"

He didn't deny it, and he didn't offer any comfort, either. But his sapphire gaze met hers evenly. "You can fix it. If you want."

She stared at him dumbfounded. "How do you figure?"

"All you have to do is realize that Hallie doesn't run away to be alone. She runs away so someone will come after her."

"Jason, if she wanted someone to come after her she wouldn't be running away in the middle of the night."

"She's six, Angie. Time has little meaning for her. Logic even less. Trust me. She ran away so that someone would come after her." He stood quietly, watching her as if he were waiting for her to draw the conclusion he was obviously trying to lead her to.

She didn't get it. Her heart ached so badly she could

barely think beyond it. Her brain was numb. He was going to have to spell it out. "And?" she prompted.

He waved a hand down his body, indicating his legs and his cane. "She knew it wasn't going to be me."

Oh God. She looked toward the staircase as she drew a deep breath and let it out slowly. "What am I going to say to her?"

"What do you want to say to her?"

What indeed? "I'm sorry."

"That's always a good place to start. Just be sure you don't tack on, 'it was my fault you ran away.'"

She looked back to him with a weary smile. "Very funny."

He smiled back unabashedly and gave her a gentle nudge toward the stairs. "Go on. I'll give you a few minutes, and then I'll be up with a couple of rice bags to warm your feet."

Chapter Fourteen

Angie walked down the hall toward Hallie's room, shivering in Jason's robe. Now that the adrenaline rush was over, she realized just how cold she was. Her legs and feet, along with the bottom of the robe, were soaking wet. The stone floors felt like ice under her bare toes.

She wanted nothing more than to crawl into a nice warm bed. But first she had to make amends with Hallie. She strode past the door leading to Dodge and looked in the open door leading to the pink palace.

Hallie had apparently switched on the light by the bed when she'd first come in, because its soft light lit the room. Hallie had already pulled off her wet clothes and was now pulling the T-shirt Jason had given her for a nightshirt over her head.

Angie leaned against the door jam. "Hey, Hallie."

At the sound of Angie's voice the little girl turned her

head around, glaring at Angie over her shoulder. "Go away."

Angie shook her head. "Sorry, can't do, kiddo. We have to talk."

"Talk, talk, talk," Hallie said, bobbing her head back and forth like an angry parrot. "That's all grown-ups do."

Under different circumstances Angie might have smiled at the juvenile petulance. But the anger was only masking Hallie's pain. And she'd put that pain there. No laughing matter. She met Hallie's angry glare head on. "Sometimes we grown-ups have something important to say."

"Like what?" Hallie snapped.

"Like I'm sorry."

A tiny spark of hope glinted in Hallie's green eyes. But it was quickly overshadowed by suspicion. "What are you sorry about? That I made you run out in the snow?"

Angie shook her head. "I'm sorry I made you sad."

"You didn't make me sad," Hallie said, her chin shooting to a defiant angle.

Angie ignored the show of bravado. It was a protective gesture she'd used often enough herself to mask a pain she didn't want anyone else to see. "Yes I did. And I'm sorry about it."

The chin tipped higher. "Why?"

"Because out of all the little children I know—and I know lots—you're the sweetest little girl in the bunch. And the last thing in the world I'd want is to make you sad."

That ray of hope got a little brighter, but Hallie was no pushover. She snorted in disbelief. "If I was the sweetest, how come you wouldn't come out of your room?"

Angie scrambled to explain the unexplainable. How could she tell a child desperate for parents that she was afraid of getting too close for fear she'd want to bring her home—when she knew she couldn't, without the child interpreting it as, I want a child, but you're not good enough for me.

Her knee-jerk reaction was to explain her absence with a lie. Again. But Hallie had seen right through her I-have-to-work ploy. There was no reason to think she wouldn't see through a second lie just as easily.

Only the truth was going to save them now. Angie rubbed her arms, not sure whether she was trying to warm herself or bolster her nerve. Stopping the motion, she looked straight into Hallie's eyes. "I'm afraid I'm not very good at leaving friends behind. I thought if I didn't get to be your friend, it wouldn't hurt when I left."

Hallie scowled at her. "That's stupid."

Yes. She just hadn't realized until tonight how stupid. She wasn't trying to make Hallie feel better when she'd said she was the sweetest little girl she knew. She *was* the sweetest kid she knew. And leaving was going to hurt. Period. Staying away hadn't saved anyone. And it had hurt Hallie deeply.

She took a breath and let it out slowly. "Oh, Hallie, have you ever goofed something up? Just totally made a mess of everything?"

Hallie stared at her, those green eyes penetrating as she considered Angie's question. Considered whether or not Angie was telling her the truth or just making up another story.

Angie held her breath.

Slowly Hallie's chin came down out of the air, the anger in her face softening. She glanced around the room as if to make sure no one was listening, then she lowered her voice to a conspiratorial whisper. "I broke Ms. Carmichael's favorite flower vase once. Her mother gave it to her and she's dead so she can't give her another. Ms.

Carmichael was very sad." Hallie's lips twisted. She obviously still felt badly about breaking the vase.

Angie nodded. "Yeah, like that. I goofed up, kiddo. Totally, one-hundred percent, without a doubt, goofed up. I was so worried about how I would feel when I had to leave, I didn't think about how my staying away would make you feel."

Hallie's eyes darted to the floor. "It made me feel bad." The words were a mere whisper.

Tears stung Angie's eyes. "I know. And I am so, so sorry." She walked across the room and gently pulled the little girl to her. She kept her grip light, giving Hallie the choice to come or not.

But the little girl came easily, her tiny arms going around Angie's hips and squeezing tight.

Angie hugged her back and then rubbed her hands comfortingly over Hallie's back. "Should we make up for lost time and my stupidity? Wanna spend tomorrow exploring the mansion together? See if we can find some lost treasures?"

Hallie looked up, her lips twitching toward a smile, but hesitation kept the smile from full bloom. "You sure you want to? I don't want you to be sad, either."

More tears sprang to Angie's eyes, and she had to quickly wipe one away before it spilled. "Hallie, I would love to spend tomorrow with you. And if you would have me, I would, very, very much like to be your friend."

Those Cupid's lips curved into a brilliant smile. "Yeah, best friends, like me and Camilla."

Angie nodded, smiling herself. "Best friends." She hugged the tiny body again.

Hallie shivered against her.

Angie shook her head, gently pushing the little girl away. "What's wrong with me? I'm soaking wet and soaking you in the bargain. Not to mention we're both freezing to death here. Let's get you into bed where you can warm up.''

Angie made quick work of getting Hallie into bed and getting her tucked under the thick, feather comforter. "Better?"

Hallie nodded. "Some. But it would be even warmer if you got in, too," she added slyly.

Angie looked at her hopeful expression. There was no running away from this one. And surprisingly, she found she didn't want to. "Yeah, it would be. Hold on." She sprinted across the hall to Jason's room, shucked the wet robe and pulled on her sweater and panties. Hurrying back to the pink palace, she dove under the covers with Hallie.

Hallie snuggled close and then shivered in reaction. "You're freezing."

Angie laughed. "Don't complain. You're no wood-burning stove, either."

Hallie giggled and snuggled closer.

"Hi ladies, I brought rice bags."

Jason's voice startled both of them and they looked in unison toward the door.

He walked in, supporting his bad leg with his cane and holding up the narrow, cotton bags filled with rice with the other hand.

Angie recognized the bags one tossed in the microwave and heated up. The twenty-first century's answer to the hot brick.

"Perfect timing. Toss those over. My feet feel like ice-bergs." Angie sat up and caught the bags Jason tossed to her. She handed one to Hallie and wrapped the second around her feet beneath the comforters. She closed her eyes as the welcome heat soaked into her toes. "Ahhh."

Jason chuckled. "You two look as snug as a couple of bugs in a rug."

Hallie giggled next to her, squirming under the covers. "We are. Want to read us a story?"

Angie's heart hitched and she waited for the panic to set in. She hadn't been able to bear listening to Jason read Hallie her bedtime story since the little girl had arrived. But the panic didn't come. An odd sort of contentment stole through her veins instead. "Yeah, Jason. Read us a story."

Jason cocked a knowing brow at her entreaty. And then a slow, satisfied smile turned his lips. "You got it." He fetched the leather-bound edition of Tom Sawyer from the dresser, pulled the plush pink chair underneath the one lamp that burned in the room, sat down and began reading.

Angie lay back down, snuggling with Hallie under the covers. Jason's rough voice settled over them as he recounted the wild tales and mischievous antics of Tom Sawyer and Huckleberry Finn. Slowly Hallie's body relaxed against hers, her breathing evening out, her baby-soft skin heating up as her body threw off the chill from her mad dash outside.

Angie glanced down at the little girl lying so heavily in her arms. Long dark lashes lay against ivory cheeks. She looked back at Jason. "She's asleep," she whispered.

Jason looked up from his reading. "Good. She needs it. She's had quite a night."

And so had they. Both before Hallie had made her great escape as well as after. Just thinking of the hours they'd spent worshipping each other's bodies made her skin blush with heat. She wanted to return to Jason's arms, but she wanted to stay here, too.

She looked at Jason, hoping he wouldn't be offended

by what she was about to ask. "Do you mind if I stay here? I don't want her to be alone if she wakes up."

Jason shook his head and smiled. "Good idea." He pushed to his feet, placed the book on the dresser and returned to the bed. He waved his hand in a shooing gesture. "Scoot over."

She tipped her head in question, but scooted over nonetheless.

Jason grabbed the pink afghan folded over the back of the chair, flicked off the light and crawled into the bed with them. "Turn over and spoon her."

Angie flipped on her side, her back to Jason, Hallie tucked carefully in front of her.

Staying on top of the covers, Jason scooted up close behind her, spread the afghan over himself and then wrapped them both in his arms. "Go to sleep." The words whispered over her nape just before his lips dropped a soft, gentle kiss on the sensitive site.

A single tear slipped over Angie's temple and caught in the pillow beneath her head. Is this what it was like to be a family? A husband snuggled behind his wife. A child held tight in her mother's arms. Is this what that drunk had stolen from her five years ago?

She stifled the cry welling up in her chest. She didn't want to upset Jason. She didn't want another confrontation tonight. She just wanted this. This one night of familial unity.

This one piece of blissful normality.

"Are you sure there're no ghosts up here?"

Angie smiled as she climbed the twisting, narrow staircase leading to one of the mansion's many attics. She'd faxed her story early this morning and, after another hearty breakfast of animal pancakes, Jason had retired to his office to work and she and Hallie had headed up here for a little exploring. "I think we're pretty safe. After all it's daytime, and I think ghosts only come out at night."

"Who says?" Hallie asked, grasping the back of Angie's sweater, making sure Angie didn't get too far ahead on the narrow stairs.

Good question. "I don't know. I must have read it somewhere."

"Ms. Carmichael says not to believe everything you read."

Angie peeked over her shoulder at the worried warning. Apprehension pulled Hallie's brows low, but excitement far outweighed the worry in her little face. In fact, Angie suspected that the idea of encountering a spectral entity was feeding the excitement.

It certainly had fed her own exhilaration when she'd been a little girl making her way to her grandmother's attic. A wry smile pulled at her lips. When she was little? Even now her heart beat faster, the adrenaline ran harder, as she imagined a see-through floating entity waiting around the next corner—and she knew better. "Well, we'll have to keep our eyes peeled then."

Another hand clamped on the back of her sweater. "Yeah. When are we going to be there?"

Angie chuckled. "Soon, I think. We've been climbing forever. Sure you don't want to just head back downstairs and play outside? We could make snowmen now that the storm is past."

"Lost treasure," Hallie stated adamantly.

"Okay then. Look out ghosts, here we come." Angie climbed the steps leading around the next sharp turn in the staircase. And there it was. Three more steps up, and the attic door awaited.

"We're here." Angie climbed the last three steps, Hallie clinging to her sweater. Turning the knob, she pushed the door open. Nothing but blackness stretched before them.

Hallie snuggled up behind her, peeking around her side, a little shiver running through her. "The ghosts will never know it's daytime up here."

Angie laughed, feeling around the stone wall next to the door. "Jason said there was a light switch right—" Finding the modern day switch, she flipped it on. "Here."

Dim light lit the long, wide room.

"Wow," Hallie breathed.

Wow indeed. The room was about a thousand times bigger than any attic she'd ever seen. Running on top of the hall that housed the pink palace, Dodge and Jason's bedroom this room was a good forty feet across and an easy sixty feet long. And unlike her grandmother's attic, which was filled with interesting but not unusual items, this one appeared to be filled with treasures both fascinating and unique.

"We've hit the jackpot, Hallie girl. If we don't find lost treasure here, or at least forgotten treasure, we're a pitiful pair." Angie stepped up into the room, Hallie close on her heels.

Unlike the ceilings in the rest of the mansion, the ceiling here didn't soar above their heads. It was low, about seven feet at the sides, and reaching to about ten feet at the center point. And it was made of giant, roughly hewn wooden beams as opposed to stone. Several dividing walls reached out from both sides of the room to help support the massive ceiling. The resulting effect was that of a giant warehouse with dozens of partitioned-off "rooms" where items could be stored without worry of everything turning into one giant jumble.

All the items in the attic had been stored quite neatly

in the spacious compartments running along both sides of the room, leaving an open walkway down the middle, and everything appeared to be stored in specific groups. Furniture in the first several partitions, then a bunch of trunks, followed by what looked like a ton of pictures and on and on and on.

"What are we looking for?" Hallie asked, coming out from behind Angie, her eyes as big as saucers as she looked at the abundance before them.

"Nothing in particular, we're just snooping. Jason said that this stuff had been collected by the owners of the mansion since it was built. Apparently, the guy who moved the house here bought everything within its walls and moved the whole lot here with the house. Who knows what we might find?"

Hallie scampered into an alcove containing furniture, her green eyes twinkling, as she darted in and out of the small spaces between the big, heavy pieces with their intricately carved surfaces and richly upholstered seats.

Angie smiled as she watched the young girl. All thoughts of ghosts had obviously fled in the wake of the adventure.

Hallie crawled onto a big, thronelike chair made of dark, ornately carved wood, a small cloud of dust springing into the air as she plopped her tiny butt down on the ragged, upholstered seat. "Think there are any toys up here?"

"I don't know. It looks like there's everything else up here. We'll have to look."

Hallie hopped down off the chair and darted back into the aisle. "I like that chair. Do you think Jason will let me put it in my room? Just till I go back."

Angie eyed the chair. It must weigh a hundred pounds.

"I don't know if we could get that chair to your room. But you could ask."

"Okay, let's look for toys." Dismissing the chair, she headed down the aisle, glancing into the side compartments for something that would interest a child more than eight-hundred-year-old furniture.

Angie watched Hallie's erratic race down the aisle and noticed the small footprints appearing in the dusty floor behind her. How many times had she dreamed of sharing days just like this with a little girl of her own? Lord, it was going to hurt when the plows made it up the road and she had to say goodbye.

But she wasn't going to let herself think about that today. Not today. She ruthlessly squelched the melancholy feelings and watched Hallie zip around the next partition to see what lay behind it.

Suddenly, the little girl jumped back with a high-pitched scream and raced back to Angie.

Angie managed to keep from being bowled over as the little girl plowed into her and then scrambled around behind her. Chuckling softly, Angie leaned forward trying to see what was behind the wall, but she was too far away. "What's back there?"

Hallie wiggled against her, her hands tightening their hold on Angie's waist. "Monsters."

"Oh yeah? Let's go see." Angie tiptoed toward the wall with Hallie glued to her backside.

Dragging the moment out, letting the suspense build, Angie slowly peeked around the short supporting wall. And nearly jumped out of her own skin. Two hideous faces glared at her from the shadows.

Reality sank in and Angie laughed in relief. "Oh geez, they got us."

"Who are they?" Hallie whispered.

"Come on, I'll show you." Still chuckling at her own gullibility, Angie stepped around the wall, dragging the reluctant Hallie with her. "Relax, they're just wooden statues."

"Statues?" Pure skepticism sounded in Hallie's voice.

"Yep. See?" Angie pointed to the two life-size gargoyles, complete from the top of their macabre, unworldly heads right down to their gnarled little toes. "It's just that at first glance, with them being hidden back there in the shadows, they look real. But they're not."

Hallie pushed her toward the statues. "Go touch one."

Angie laughed as Hallie offered her up to the goblins. "Don't believe me, huh?" Walking up to the statues, she reached out and rapped her knuckles sharply on one, the hollow sound of wood resonating around them. "See? Just wood."

Hallie's brows pulled low. "I don't want to touch them. They look mean."

Angie shook her head. "They're the good guys. They're all over the castle, remember? There's one carved on the mantel over the fire in the study. There's one in your room up in one of the corners."

Hallie nodded. "I seen 'em. Who are they?"

"The gargoyles."

Hallie made a face. "Why are they all over the house? They look mean."

"They're supposed to look mean, but they're the good guys. Jason says they guard the house and the people who live here. Their job is to keep all the bad guys away and make sure nothing happens to the house's family."

Hallie's face scrunched up skeptically. "Do you believe that?"

Angie started to shake her head no, started to say it was all folklore. But then she remembered the gargoyle crashing to the floor in Jason's room last night—crashing to the floor and waking them up just in time for them to hear Hallie make her escape. And she remembered how the gargoyle had seemed so fierce when he'd perched in the corner of the room chomping on his war prize. His face would have scared any intelligent interloper away, but when she'd picked him up from the floor, he'd only appeared worried.

She shrugged her shoulder. "Maybe."

Surprise widened Hallie's green eyes. "Really?"

Angie nodded. "Really."

Hallie moved closer to the big wooden statues. Tentatively she reached out and touched one. When it didn't bite she moved closer, running her hand over its dry, smooth surface. She turned to Angie with her brows pulled low, her expression most serious. "I don't think they should be up here."

"Why not?"

"'Cause nobody ever comes up to visit them here. They must be very lonely." Her brows pulled together in grave concern. "I think they should be downstairs where we can visit them more often."

Oh dear. The yaks again.

But the last time she'd changed something in this house—opening the shutters—Jason had been furious. Of course, she could maybe avoid that scene if she just ran down and asked Jason if they could move the beasts.

But what if he said no?

Hallie would be disappointed—again—and these poor gargoyles would be consigned to another eight hundred years of dust and darkness.

And surely, even if Jason were angry, he wouldn't yell at Hallie. He might very well strangle Angie after he'd shipped Hallie off to some other part of the mansion to watch TV or color pictures, but he would never lose his temper with the little girl. Particularly once he realized that Hallie was just trying to save the poor, sad monsters from loneliness.

Angie blew the layer of dust from one of the wide, animal-like noses. "Where do you think would be a good place for them?"

Hallie gave it serious thought. "Maybe by the front door. That's where the bad guys would come in."

"Good idea." Angie mentally chuckled. That barren room could use a few friendly, and even not-so-friendly, faces. As a matter of fact…

"You know, Hallie, that room isn't really much cozier than this one. What do you say we bring a few other things down to make them comfortable. Like…" She looked around the attic, her gaze coming to rest on a pile of rolled carpets. "A rug or two."

Hallie's green eyes sparkled at the idea. "Yeah. Let's fix the whole room up for them. Some rugs and pitchers and…" She spun around, looking at the attic's contents. "Do you think they would like a chair to sit on?"

"Oh yeah, I think they would definitely like a chair to sit on." She was eager to save the gargoyles from loneliness and bring some warmth to the barren foyer, but mostly she wanted to leave her mark in Jason's house.

The fates had conspired against her, bringing Jason into her life, knowing full well she'd never be able to share more than these few days with him. But damn it, she didn't want him to forget her. She wanted him to remember. And by golly, she was going to do her best to make him remember—every time he walked through his entrance hall.

"Okay, Hallie girl, let's get busy. I'll drag some rugs

down, and you can start going through the pictures. Okay?''

Hallie nodded her understanding. ''Okay. But I want to help pick out the rugs first.''

''All righty. But you have to pick them out of the top five or six. Getting one or two of them downstairs is going to kill me as it is. I'm not going to pull that whole pile apart. Got it?''

''Got it.'' Hallie nodded once and scampered over to the pile of colorful rugs.

The next couple of hours flew by like birds on the wing. To their surprise, Jason did not so much as peek out of his office as they transformed his sterile entrance into…well, something quite different.

First, they used the two rugs Hallie picked out to ease the gargoyles down the two staircases, one careful stair at a time. Then they spent hours digging through the plethora of pictures upstairs. Finally they dusted and dragged down five pastoral landscapes with an assortment of animals dotting the peaceful, rolling hillsides.

And now they were carefully dragging down the giant chair Hallie had originally wanted in her room.

Suddenly, Jason's office door swung open and he strode out into the foyer, his cane tapping on the stone. ''What is going on out here? You two are making enough noise to wake the dead.'' He stopped in his tracks, his gaze flying over the room and its new appointments.

First, he encountered the two rugs, one at the bottom of each of the staircases, then, the pictures that had been leaned against the walls at various intervals, since she and Hallie had no way to hang them, and the giant chair lying at her feet. Finally his gaze landed on the gargoyles flanking the door.

Angie held her breath, waiting to see if he'd be as angry about this as he had been about the windows.

But when he looked back to her, a brilliant smile turned his lips. "I like it."

Hallie jumped up and down, squealing her delight at his approval. Then she raced across the foyer to the gargoyles, giving one a hearty pat. "They were lonely up there in the attic, so I thought they should come down here."

"And so they should. And you've found the perfect spot for them, too. They look quite content there."

Surprise zipped through Angie at his obvious pleasure. She'd expected he might be angry about the change in his home, or if they were lucky, merely complacent. But pleased? She raised a brow.

He switched his attention to her, a smile turning his lips. "I love it."

She tilted her head, watching him. He looked as if he meant it, not as if he was merely mouthing platitudes to make Hallie happy. "I was a little nervous, thinking about how you disapproved of me opening your shutters."

He met her gaze head on. "Well, as someone I have the utmost regard for recently pointed out to me, one can only cry in his beer and throw so many pity parties before the act becomes a mockery of itself. It's time to move on. As a matter of fact, I found the perfect property for the next Kent House." He shot her a triumphant smile. "And I just bought it."

"You *bought* it? That's why you stayed locked away in your office even with us making so much racket out here?"

He nodded.

Joy stole through her veins, and she had to blink to keep the sudden tears stinging her eyes from spilling over.

"I guess that means you aren't waiting to see if the kids give you their blessing."

He shook his head. "I'll work something out. If I'm too much for the kids, I'll hire someone who isn't. Or I'll think of some other way. But there will be a way."

Right now, right at this instant, she was so proud of him, and so thrilled for him, she could burst. She sent him a beaming smile. "Congratulations. Where's the new home going to be?"

"Rock Creek. About a hundred miles from here. Close enough that I can keep an eye on it." He smiled at her, letting her know how glad he was that she'd pushed him to make the decision. "I think this calls for a celebration."

"Yeah!" Hallie screamed, racing back from the gargoyles. "Let's celebrate! Do you have a cake in the freezer? Ms. Carmichael always keeps a cake in the freezer for special 'cassions."

He grabbed her hand and started toward the kitchen. "Sorry, no cake. But I bet we can find something. Let's go look."

Angie watched them walk away, her heart squeezing in her chest. Jason was moving on to his dream. She was happy for him. But the fact that she could never be the woman to share that dream with him sliced at her heart. And the fact that the three of them would have to go their separate ways in just a few days hurt even more.

But she wasn't going to let those dark thoughts ruin what little time they had left together. This moment was precious, and she intended to relish it and savor it and remember it for all the lonely days ahead.

Halfway across the foyer, Jason stopped and turned to her with a pointed look. "You are coming, aren't you?"

She shook herself out of her reverie and gave him an easy grin. "You bet I am."

Chapter Fifteen

Jason sat on the floor next to the coffee table in the study, sipping his hot cocoa and studying the chessboard in front of him. Angie and Hallie were killing him. He mentally shook his head. Three-sided chess, who'da thought? But the made-up game had its own charms and it was making the evening every bit as much fun as the day had been. And he couldn't remember when he'd enjoyed a day more.

Having made the decision to open another Kent House had made him feel as though he'd finally opened the door on the black pit he'd been in for the last three years. And celebrating the decision with Angie and Hallie had been…perfect.

As perfect as the last two nights with Angie had been.

It seemed to him, sitting here, that he was as close to heaven as he was ever going to get. A beautiful, passionate woman sitting to his left. A cute-as-a-pixie girl sitting across from him. It was as though they were a real family.

They weren't, of course. Nothing about the scene was real. When the plows made it up the road, it would all disappear. But he wouldn't let himself think about that. The bitterness, the pain, the hopelessness of the last three years were too close.

The excitement he'd felt when he bought the property for the new Kent House this afternoon made him realize how right Angie had been. He'd wasted the last three years of his life. But still, he didn't have to look too deep in his heart to wonder whether going back to work would be enough, whether it would keep the black emptiness of the last three years at bay.

It wasn't a job that he'd dreamed about while he was growing up, or fought so hard for during the last fifteen years of his life. It was a wife and children, a family and a home. And it was the absence of those, knowing he'd never have *them*, that had almost sent him over the edge. And that pit, deep and cold and dark, still waited for him.

So he didn't let himself think about tomorrow or the next day when the plows might make it up his road. Angie and Hallie were here now. And, although Angie couldn't face his infirmities during the day, she was happy to accept his comfort at night. Heaven simply wasn't going to get closer than this.

He took another sip of hot cocoa and studied the board before him, remembering the rules they'd come up with as he planned his strategy. The objective in three-sided chess was a little different than in the real game. Here the main objective was simply to get all the other guys' pieces. The player with the most captured pieces at the end of the game won.

The rules, however, were vaguely the same. Each piece

had to move as it did in the original game, but the placing was definitely different. Each player fanned his pieces out from their corner of the playing field in small triangles, three players deep.

Hallie had all the white major players; Angie, the black. He had all the pawns—twice as many players, but with very little maneuverability. That, and the fact that the girls had ganged up on him, meant his pieces were dropping like flies. He took another sip of cocoa and conceded that at this stage of the game, strategy was useless. Defeat was imminent.

But he wasn't going down without a fight. He captured Angie's king as he moved his pawn forward a square. A small victory, but one of the few he was likely to get.

Angie narrowed her eyes. "I'll get you for that."

He rolled his eyes. "I'm sure you will. You and your short cohort." He sent Hallie a teasing glance.

"I'm not short," Hallie giggled on the other side of the table. "But I'm mean." And with those words she slid her bishop across the board with blood lust sparkling in her eyes, toppling yet another of the humble pawns that Angie had previously blocked so the little mite could swoop in and snatch it away.

Scooping the small alabaster pawn into her hand, Hallie held it above her head in triumph. "Gotcha again."

He shot her a mock scowl. "I think we should amend the rules. No ganging up on the owner of the chessboard."

But Hallie only giggled harder, shaking her head vigorously, long black curls flying everywhere. "Girls against boys, that's how we play at Kent House all the time."

He raised a brow. "I'll have to speak to Ms. Carmichael about that. Not only is it politically incorrect, it's bloody inconvenient at the moment."

Angie swooped in and took another of his defenseless pawns with her black knight and a wicked laugh. "It's been girls against boys and boys against girls since the beginning of time, soldier. Live with it."

He cocked his head and gave her a heated, sideways glance. "Careful. I'm keeping track. And tonight it will be the boys against the girls."

Her cheeks blushed pink, but the sultry gaze she sent his way was anything but innocent. "That's okay. The girls figured out a long time ago that with the right boy...losing is every bit as good as winning." Underneath the table, where Hallie couldn't see, she stroked her bare foot slowly up his thigh. Up his thigh and into his lap. "Maybe even better."

He hardened against the sole of her foot, fast and needy. And, when he pictured her bare foot with its sexy red toenails snuggled against the boldest part of him, he had to stifle a groan.

"Your turn, Jason. Hurry up." Hallie bounced up and down on her knees, sharply reminding him there was nothing he could do about the fire racing through his blood. At least not until later.

He tried to pull himself out of the sexual fog clogging his brain. "Give—" He had to stop and clear an entire battalion of frogs out of his throat. "Give me a minute, I'm thinking."

With a cheeky, self-satisfied grin, Angie pulled her foot out of his lap and resettled herself as primly as a school-marm at her end of the table.

Yeah, he'd get her for that later. But right now he tried to rearrange his scrambled thoughts. Picking up the first pawn he spotted, he moved it forward a square.

Right in front of Hallie's rook.

Damn.

Hallie wasted no time in swooping down on the poor fellow, knocking him down and snatching him up like the bloodthirsty little general she was. "You're not thinking very good," she crowed.

He shot Angie a wry look. "No kidding."

Angie laughed unsympathetically, and Hallie joined in as she added the pawn to her growing pile.

He shook his head and laughed, too, savoring every minute of the easy teasing and shared camaraderie.

It was Angie's turn next and she smugly captured his next-to-last piece with her freewheeling queen. Exacting what revenge he could, he took Hallie's knight with his last remaining man and then calmly awaited defeat.

Which Hallie delivered with great enthusiasm. Snagging his last warrior with her king, the most coveted but least effective piece on the board, she held it high above her head. "I win!"

Jason groaned. Beaten by a six-year-old. "I want a rematch." Realizing how late it was and wanting to drag Angie off so that she could pick up where she'd left off, he amended, "Tomorrow night."

"Yeah, tomorrow night." Hallie's eyes sparkled with excitement and she bounced up and down on her knees. "I want to do it every night. I think you should marry Angie and you should both adopt me and we could be a family forever and ever."

His heart stopped. Just stopped. And then started again with a slow, painful ache. He would sell his soul to be able to fulfill the hope in Hallie's eyes, to be able to meet the answering need in his own heart. But he couldn't do it. It wasn't within his power.

He glanced at Angie. She was pale as a ghost, panic flashing in her eyes. He knew what was going on in her mind, knew she was blaming herself for Hallie's hope.

Knew she was thinking everyone would have been better off if they'd just stayed the hell away from each other.

The earth shifted beneath him. Shifted and began to shatter. Again. If he didn't do something fast, it would all be over. And he wasn't ready for it to end. Not yet.

He looked over at Hallie. "I think that's a decision that is going to take quite a bit of thought, little one. And right now it's bedtime. Let's get you upstairs and tucked in so you're plenty rested for making snowmen tomorrow, okay?"

The light faded out of Hallie's eyes, her excited expression crumpling before his eyes. She knew a brush-off when she heard one.

His heart squeezed. How many times had prospective parents come to the orphanage when he was young? Couples he'd hoped would bring him home. And how many times had they left with another little boy? One younger or cuter or smarter than he had been. Too many times. Too many painful times.

Damn.

He'd give his one good knee for a magic wand that could make them all the family Hallie wished them to be. The family *he* wanted them to be. But it was a useless wish, a futile hope. "Come on, sweetie, let's get you tucked in."

Hallie pushed herself to her feet, her lips trembling as she did her best to hide her disappointment. "Okay." The words were whisper thin as she walked over to Angie and gave her a big hug. "'Night."

Angie hugged her back, her eyes closed tight as if she were fighting back tears. And Jason imagined she was. He knew she wanted children, knew she was denying that desire for some reason she wouldn't share. But to have Hallie all but begging for her love and to have to withhold it, when he knew she desperately wanted to give it, had to be tearing Angie's heart to shreds. Lord knew, it was slashing at his.

He pushed himself up from the floor and grabbed his cane, trying to breathe through the ache in his chest.

Hallie pushed away from Angie. "You going to tuck me, too?"

Angie shook her head, swiping away a tear that spilled over her lash. "I think I'll let Jason do that tonight. I better stay down here and clean up this mess." Her voice was rough as she waved a hand over the coffee table.

"Okay. See ya tomorrow." Hallie turned from Angie and took Jason's hand, her chin wobbling as she did her best to keep from crying.

He led her out of the study, his heart pounding in his chest, frustration racing through his veins. He wanted to strangle someone. He just didn't know who. Angie, for hiding behind her damned walls with her fears and pain and giving him absolutely nothing to fight them with? The guerilla for keeping him near the explosion that had made him acceptable for a short-term affair but unacceptable for a long-term commitment? God, for saddling Hallie with a bad heart and then ripping her parents away from her? Or the fates, for throwing them all together when there wasn't a hope in hell of them staying that way?

He took Hallie up to her bedroom, helped her change into his T-shirt and tucked her into bed, his heart aching at the sadness in her green eyes. He pulled the covers tight around her ears. "Sleep well now." He leaned down and placed a kiss on the tiny forehead, wishing it could be a promise of future happiness.

"'Night." Tears glistened in Hallie's eyes as she gave him one last hug.

His throat closed up, making it almost impossible to

breathe. "'Night," he whispered back, pushing the word past the constriction in his throat. Pulling the chain on the lamp, he plunged the room into darkness, a darkness that pounded at his soul, reminding him of the abyss that waited just around the corner.

He slipped out of the room and pulled the door shut behind him. Leaning against the cool oak panel, he fought the wave of panic rushing over him.

You love them.

He closed his eyes against the all-too-familiar voice and tried to deny the statement. But it was useless. It pounded in his head and in his heart with the undeniable power of simple truth.

If you don't do something fast, you're going to lose them both.

Shut up.

Oh yeah, that'll fix it.

Nothing will fix it. For all my preaching about one-parent households, Hallie deserves two parents. And no matter what my feelings for Angie are, she isn't interested in hooking up with a cripple.

It doesn't seem to bother her that you're a cripple when she's in bed with you.

Have you forgotten she demands that I turn out the lights?

No. I'm just saying that when she's in your arms, when you're making love to her, when she's making love to you, there's an intensity to it, an honesty about it, that makes me doubt your assessment.

So what?

So quit leaning against this door like some loser door knocker and fight for what you want. At the very least if you're going to let the lady walk out of your life, make her tell you to your face why she's doing it.

Yeah, that sounds like fun. He scrubbed his hand down his face, his gut clenching at the mere prospect of the confrontation. But the voice, coming straight from his heart, was right, this was the deciding moment. He'd seen the look on Angie's face when he'd taken Hallie out of the study. If she had her way, she'd lock herself in her bedroom away from them both until the plows came up the road.

The question was, was he going to let her?

Was he going to let her walk out of his life as easily as she'd walked into it?

Not a chance in hell.

Jason leaned against the wall next to the stairs and waited for Angie to come up. She wouldn't be long. How much time could it take to pick up the chessboard and put three mugs away, even if she washed them? Ten minutes tops. And he'd spent eight of those minutes tucking Hallie in.

Even as he thought it, Angie's footsteps echoed up the wide staircase into the hall. She was on her way.

Because the hallway led off the stairs to the right, she didn't see him until she hit the top of the landing and turned down the hall. She jumped when she saw him leaning there.

"Sorry. Didn't mean to startle you."

She took one look at him leaning against the wall and her lips turned down. "No, just waylay me."

Little point in denying it. He gave her a single nod. "We need to talk."

She plowed her fingers through her hair, agitation marring her brow. "There's nothing to talk about, Jason. We can't do this anymore."

It's what he had expected her to say. That or something

similar. In the study he'd known she was shutting herself away. But she wasn't getting off the hook that easily. In fact, if he had his way, she wasn't getting off the hook at all. "Do you want to clarify what 'this' is?"

"You know what 'this' is." Anger flashed in her eyes as she waved a hand toward Hallie's door and then toward the door leading to his bedroom. "Can't you see that Hallie has sensed we've gotten closer in the last few days, and she's made us the mommy and daddy in her own fairy tale. We can't keep encouraging her ideas, Jason. Not when we know what we're sharing isn't going anywhere. It's not fair."

They'd gotten to the crux of the matter more quickly than he had anticipated. Maybe more quickly than he wanted. Just standing here in the hall with her, the scent of jasmine filling his senses, the soft surface of her skin within touching distance, was better than having her locked in her room where he couldn't see her, couldn't draw her sweet scent in, couldn't touch her. And if this conversation didn't go the way he wanted, she'd be out of his reach forever.

But there was no way to postpone this confrontation any longer. If he didn't stop her now, she'd disappear into her room anyway. And she was right, if there was no more between them than a few nights of shared pleasure, continuing wouldn't be good for Hallie.

But he was not going into that dark night gently.

He pushed away from the wall and closed the distance between them until he could feel her heat soaking into him. Until he knew she was feeling his heat soaking into her. "I'm not going to beat around the bush here, Angie, or hide behind ambiguous metaphors. I'm just going to lay it all out on the table."

He paused briefly, drawing a deep breath and gathering

his nerve. And then he jumped in with both feet and all his heart. "When I hold you in my arms at night, I feel like the world is what it should be. Good and wonderful and bright. And if you want me to walk away from that without a fight, you're going to have to tell me why you think what we've shared for the last two nights can't go anywhere. Because it sure as hell feels like it could go somewhere to me."

Something suspiciously like yearning flashed in her eyes. But he hardly had time to recognize it before panic crashed over it. She spun away from him, her hands opening and closing in agitation.

His gut clenched as he waited.

When she turned back to him pain and frustration filled her eyes. "You're making this a hundred times harder than it has to be. Can't you just accept that it's over?"

"If you want to put an end to it, Angie, you're going to have to tell me why. You're going to have to say it."

Her brows drew together. "Say what?"

"Say you're not interested in getting involved full-time with a scarred cripple."

She reeled back, her mouth dropping open, her eyes going wide. And then the shock turned to hurt. "After the last two nights, how could you possibly think that?"

He met her gaze squarely. "What else am I to think? You're happy in my arms as long as the lights are off and you don't have to face the reality of who I am."

"Oh God." Pain and regret filled her expression as she closed the distance between them. "You thought I wanted the lights off so I wouldn't see your scars?"

"Wasn't that the reason?"

"Never," she whispered, bringing her hand to his face and cupping his jaw. "I love your scars. Every one of them." She brought her lips to his cheek—to his scar, and rained tiny, soft kisses along the jagged line as she continued to whisper. "They're part of you. Maybe the best part of you. They tell of your courage and your honor and your sheer humanness. I love them."

He wanted to believe her. God, he wanted to believe her, but... "Then why wouldn't you let me turn on the light?"

She closed her eyes and shook her head, blocking him out. "I knew I never should have gotten involved with you. I knew this was going to have a bad end. That one of us was going to get hurt."

The words ripped at him like a sharp knife. "Then why did you?"

She opened her eyes and met his gaze. But she didn't answer him.

"Why, damn it?"

Her eyes sparked with frustration. "Because I couldn't resist you. From the moment you opened the door, I couldn't resist anything about you. Not your looks or your honor or the way you looked at me."

His heart tripped. That last statement definitely didn't sound like a woman who was overly concerned about either his scars or his bum knee. And he knew she had other issues. The trick was to find out which issues were making her want to run.

He drew a tight rein on the hope surging through him and moved ahead as carefully as a man picking his way through a mine field. "How did I look at you?" he asked softly.

Her shoulders slumped and she gave him a weary sigh. "Oh, Jason, let's not do this. It's not going to get you what you want. And it's just going to make us sad."

He looked at the shadows in her eyes. Felt the dark

abyss creeping around the corner for him. "We're sad now."

"We're going to be sadder."

Maybe. "How did I look at you?"

Resignation filled her eyes. Color flooded her cheeks. "Like I was the most desirable woman in the world."

"And that's a bad thing?"

Tears sprang to her eyes, and she looked away, trying to hide them. "It is when you have everything to offer me, and I have nothing to offer you."

He stared at her, dumbfounded. "How do you figure that?"

She shifted restlessly on her feet, and he knew she was trying to decide whether she should finish this conversation or just run. Finally she looked back at him, tears glistening in her eyes, her chin tipped at a defensive angle. "I know what you want, Jason. And I can't give it to you."

"*What* is it you think I want?" he demanded, exasperated. "And what makes you think you can't give it to me?"

She stared at him, her lips pressed together, her eyes bright with tears. "I hate you for making me tell you this. I wanted this time to be special. I wanted to remember you looking at me the way you have for the past few days. Now all I'm going to remember is the look on your face after I tell you. And how glad you were to get rid of me then."

What the hell was she talking about? "Stop stalling, Angie, and cough it up."

The tears spilled over her lashes in a torrent now, a torrent she tried to wipe away with a shaky hand. "Children." The single word was whisper soft. "I can't give you children."

If she was saying she couldn't have children he could easily understand her pain. And his heart ached for her. But he didn't understand at all how that was supposed to change his feelings for her. "You can't have children?" he queried softly, just to be sure he was on the right track.

She shook her head, swiping at the tears.

He wanted to scoop her into his arms. But she wouldn't accept that now. In fact, he feared she'd run if he even tried to touch her. "Why can't you have children?" He kept his voice, soft, comforting. It was a hard question, but he sensed it would lead to the answers he needed.

She plowed her fingers through her hair. "What difference does it make?"

"I think it makes a great deal of difference. To you."

She shot him a disparaging look. "But not to you, right?"

He ignored the sarcasm. This was too important for him to let her bait him. "Why can't you have children?"

Her lips thinned, but she finally launched into her story. "I was on my way to pick up the wedding invitations for Steven's and my wedding when a drunk came around a blind curve and hit me head-on." Bitterness filled her words.

His gut tightened at the mere thought of her behind the wheel in a head-on collision. "How badly were you hurt?"

"On the outside, not too bad. But a lot was crushed on the inside. I was bleeding internally when the paramedics arrived. They had me airlifted to the nearest hospital where they went in to stop the bleeding. Except stopping the bleeding meant removing a few organs." Her expression filled with pain, she turned back to him. "Including my uterus."

"Oh God," he reached out to comfort her.

But she moved away, out of his reach, swiping at her tears.

He looked away, staring at the gray stone walls. And that's when it occurred to him. He looked back to her. "*That's* why you wanted the lights out. Not to avoid seeing my scars, but so I wouldn't see yours."

She nodded.

He felt horrible for her, but he could hardly miss the irony of what she was telling him. He shook his head. "We are, bar none, the two stupidest people that ever walked this planet."

She turned back to him. "What is that supposed to mean?"

He stared past her shoulder toward the end of the hall. Stared at the door leading to his bedroom. And the one leading to Hallie's. "It means we were both so fixated on what the other person didn't want—as in I thought you didn't want a cripple and you thought I didn't want someone who couldn't have kids—that neither of us could see what they *did* want."

And it was time for him to tell her *exactly* what he wanted.

Sweat breaking out on the palms of his hands, he strangled the eagle at the top of his cane. The next few seconds were crucial. He locked his gaze on hers. "I have something very important to say. And I want you to listen very carefully."

She crossed her arms over her chest, pain filling her eyes. "You needn't bother. I assure you, I've heard it all before. You have the highest regard for me. However, you always wanted a family and you need a woman who can help you fulfill that dream. And so, despite your feelings for me, you simply must move on." Those bee-stung lips formed a hard, bitter line.

Anger, white-hot and steaming, surged through him. No wonder Angie was so afraid of risking her heart again. Her fiancé had walked out on her during the toughest part of her life—walked out on her and made her feel as though she were no longer worthy of his or any other man's love.

The scum-sucking son of a bitch.

He clamped down on his anger. The only important thing right now was what he had to say to the woman in front of him. He cocked a brow at her. "Now that you've gotten that out of your system, is it my turn?"

She hugged herself tighter, but she raised her chin a notch. "Fine, go ahead."

He locked his gaze on hers, drew a deep, fortifying breath and plunged ahead. "I love you. From the top of your pretty, stubborn little head right down to your sexy little toes, I love you. And I want—"

"Stop it." Panic filled her face, and she threw her hands up in front of her as if she could stop his words with her hands. "Don't say that. You don't mean it." She backed farther away, pain and fear clouding her face.

You don't mean it. A legacy left by a man who claimed his love and then left her when she lost her perfection. The bastard better hope Jason *never* ran into him on the street. He kept his gaze locked on hers. "I mean it, Angie. Every word, every syllable, every letter."

She shook her head frantically. "No you don't. And even if you did love me right now, right this minute, it would never last. I know. I *know.* Steven loved me, too. Before the accident. And he tried to love me after, but he couldn't. And you won't be able to, either. You want a family as badly as he did."

He narrowed his eyes on her. "Don't," he warned in a deadly whisper, "compare me to that worm. In fact, if you mention his name one more time I'm going to strangle you. And then I'm going to track the weasely bastard down and strangle *him.* I *know* what I want out of life, Angie. And it's not a convenient brood mare. I want—''

''You want *children,*'' she broke in, jabbing her finger over his shoulder toward the two doors down the hall. ''And those two rooms prove it. Not that I needed proof. It's human nature. Every man wants a son to carry on his name.''

He resisted the urge to tell her he didn't want anything of the sort. But he couldn't embellish reality here. Only naked truth would carry the day. And he was desperate to carry the day. ''I do want children,'' he admitted. ''I've always wanted children. Growing up an orphan made me appreciate the simpler things in life. A roof over my head, a wife in my bed, children under my feet. It's all I've ever wanted.

''But I'm not some egotistical ass who has to have a child from my own loins to prove I'm a man. There are a million homeless children out there that I would love to call my own. There's a little girl right down there—'' he jabbed a thumb over his shoulder ''—I would sell my soul to keep. A little girl I think you would love to call your own as well.''

She closed her eyes against the suggestion, a single tear tracking down her cheek. ''It doesn't matter what I want. That's what I keep trying to tell you. I can't adopt children any more than I can have them.''

He cocked his head, studying her intently, realizing he had yet another wall to get through. ''What skewed piece of reasoning is at work to make you think that?''

''I lost a lot more than my uterus in my accident, remember? I lost a kidney and spleen, too. Do you have any idea what that means?''

"Obviously not, since I don't understand how missing a kidney and spleen could have anything to do with adopting a child."

"No spleen means my immune system is weak. A simple case of pneumonia would kill me. Even with today's antibiotics. And what happens if the one kidney I have fails? They do sometimes, you know? Just fail. For no apparent reason. Or what if I have another accident, lose the last kidney. What then? A kid who's already lost one set of parents loses another. How fair is that?"

"For crying out loud, Angie, life isn't fair. But growing up an orphan, I can tell you right now that if I'd had the chance to have a pair of loving parents for even one week, *one week,* I would have taken it and considered myself the luckiest boy on earth. Because the loss, no matter how painful, would never have outweighed the gain—knowing that for however brief a period, someone had loved me. So stop hiding behind what-ifs. A meteor could crash into the earth tomorrow and kill us all. You want to hide in the cellar and wait for that one?"

"Don't you dare compare my trying to protect some child's heart with some stupid meteor. It's not the same thing, and you know it."

"Oh yes it is. It's exactly the same thing. And I'll tell you what else is the same. This poor-poor-pitiful-me routine of yours has a striking resemblance to the pity party I've been throwing for myself the last three years."

He shook his head. "You were so damned self-righteous that night when you told me you'd made your peace with your life and moved on, while pointing out that I hadn't so much as poked my toe out of this house. Well guess what, lady? You didn't move on. You just found a different place to hide."

"How can you possibly say that? The two circumstances are *nothing* alike."

"The two circumstances are *exactly* alike. The only difference is that while I was hiding behind three-foot stone walls you were hiding behind a monthly byline. And I can say it because I know where you're coming from. I know how strong the desire to hide is. I know how easy it is to look at what you no longer have, what you can no longer do, and think that it will keep you from having the future you envisioned. But *you've* shown me how wrongheaded that thinking is."

He looked straight into her eyes. "I was positive the first time I looked in the mirror that no woman would ever look at me again. I was even more positive after a few women looked at me and turned away in horror. But then you came along. And you not only looked and didn't run away, you crawled into my bed. Most eagerly I might add."

She flushed a pretty shade of pink, but more important, the anger, and even some of the pain, faded from her eyes.

He pushed his case. He indicated his scar with his hand, then waved toward his knee. "This is what I am. This is what I have. The reality is that I will never chase my children in the snow. Or carry my bride over the threshold. But if you stay, I can promise you this. You'll have a solid, if slightly eccentric, roof over your head. Good food on the table. And you'll know from the moment you wake up in the morning until the moment you fall asleep at night that I love you. With all my heart and all my soul and all my being."

A tear spilled over her lashes. She wanted to believe him. He could see it in her eyes.

He pushed a little more. "Listen, I'm not trying to minimize what happened to you. Or pretend it might not affect your future. It might mean that you won't live as long as the next guy. But, Angie, you could just as easily live to be a hundred. So I guess the only question left is this one. Do you want to live those years alone? Or with me?''

He held his breath, his hand strangling the eagle at the top of his cane, his heart praying that she'd move beyond her fears and step into his arms.

But she just closed her eyes in misery. ''It's not that easy.''

''Damn it, it is that easy.'' Panic clutched his heart. He was going to lose her.

She shook her head. ''I have to think about it.''

His stomach plunged. She wouldn't think about it. She'd made her decision, he could see it in the pain filling her eyes. She was just tossing him a bone so she could run away. And there wasn't a damn thing he could do about it. He'd played his hand.

And lost.

A scream rent the air, high pitched and desperate.

They both whipped around to look down the hall where the scream had come from, their minds racing to the same conclusion. ''Hallie!''

Chapter Sixteen

"**O**h God." Fear slammed through Angie like a lightning bolt. She glanced back at Jason.

He grabbed her arm and propelled her toward Hallie's room. "Go," he commanded. "I'm right behind you."

She raced down the hall and slammed into Hallie's room. A cold blast of Arctic air hit her, raising goose bumps on her skin and increasing the dread pounding through her veins. She quickly scanned the room.

Empty.

But one of the side levers on the giant window stood open. Wide open, the curtains billowing fitfully as the frigid night air rushed into the room.

"Help me." The tiny cry wafted in from outside.

Her heart froze, but her feet raced to the open window. If Hallie had crawled out that window thinking she could easily gain the ground and run away, she was in big trouble. The stories on this mansion weren't anything like those on a normal house. The roof outside Hallie's window was a good twenty-five feet off the ground.

"Hallie," she called, leaning out the window and peering into the moonlit night. She spotted Hallie immediately.

She was twenty feet out on the roof's ledge, draped over one of the mansion's gargoyles, her tiny arms wrapped around the beast's neck as she clung precariously to the snow-encrusted stone.

Fear exploded in her chest. "Hold on, sweetie." Oh God, where was Jason?

She glanced over her shoulder just as he came into the room, hurrying as quickly as his leg would allow. "She's out on the ledge."

His face paled, but then the professional soldier kicked in, his face becoming a hard, emotionless mask. "Don't panic. We'll get her in." He joined her at the window, leaning out to assess the situation.

She gripped her shaking hands and tried to control her fear. "*How* are we going to get her back in?"

"I don't know yet. Give me a minute to look things over." He turned his attention to Hallie. "How ya doing out there, princess? Are you hurt anywhere?"

Hallie shook her head. "But I'm scared. It's too high. Come get me." The plaintive wail filled the icy night air.

"We're coming. But first I need you to tell me how you got out there so far."

"I climbed up the roof to the top and crawled along the point because there was no snow there. But when I tried to climb down so I could slide down the pole under the gargoyle like a fireman, I fell. The snow was too slippery." A fresh wave of crying erupted as she remembered the scary moment. "The gargoyle caught me just in time."

Angie's heart pounded in her ears as she followed the path Hallie described. She could easily see the narrow path on the steep roof right next to the bedroom window where the snow had melted because of the house's heat. It would have been easy for Hallie to climb up that dry path to the roof's pitch, which was also free of snow.

Moving along the roof's top line wouldn't have been too difficult. With a leg and arm on either side of the roof, it was the one place Hallie would have had a modicum of balance. But at six the little girl hadn't thought about how slippery the snow would be for her descent. A deep gouge in the white blanket covering the rest of the roof marked her uncontrolled slide down to the gargoyle's back. Six inches to the right or left and Hallie would have plunged to the ground.

"Are you coming to get me?" Another plaintive wail filled with tears.

"In just a minute, princess," Jason answered. "We have to get some equipment set up first, okay? Right now I want you to hold on tight to that gargoyle. Got it? Don't move. He'll take care of you."

Hallie nodded, sniffing. "Hurry up."

"We will," he reassured her before pulling himself back into the room and turning to Angie. "You're going to have to go get her. You know that, don't you?"

Her stomach dropped to her toes. "Climb out there?" Fear ran up her spine. She wasn't good with heights. Not good at all.

"Well I can't do it, damn it." Frustration filled his voice, but the second the angry words were out of his mouth he took hold of himself. He smoothed the lines of his face into his professional mask. "Angie, I can't get her. But I *can* get you out there and both of you back safely if you do what I tell you."

She closed her eyes against the panic drowning her and took hold of her disintegrating nerves. The sweetest little girl in the world was caught out on the roof far above the ground. She could do this.

And she wouldn't be doing it alone. Jason would get her through. She opened her eyes and met Jason's gaze head-on. "What do I do?"

He gave her arm a reassuring squeeze. "Good. First, I need you to run to the armory and bring back some climbing gear. Two coils of rope, a pair of crampons—"

"What are crampons?"

"They're ice cleats that strap onto the soles of your boots so you don't slip on the ice and snow. You'll know them when you see them."

She nodded.

"The rope. The crampons. And two harnesses. Got it?"

"Yep." She raced out of the room, down the hall, down the stairs, up the stairs and into the armory, fearing that every second she was away would be the one that cost Hallie her life. The climbing equipment was neatly stored on shelves to the right. She plowed into them the second she came through the door.

Angie found the ropes immediately and the crampons soon after. But finding the harnesses in the array of ropes and nylon webbing was more difficult. Urgency poured through her as she sifted through the multitude of lines. It was cold outside, Hallie was scared, anything could happen. She needed to get back. Fast.

Finally, she found the twin harnesses. She snatched them up, grabbed the rest of the equipment and sped back to Hallie's room.

Jason was leaning out the window talking to Hallie, his voice calm, comforting as she ran in.

She dumped all the gear on the bed. "How's she doing?"

He glanced over his shoulder at her and then turned back to Hallie. "Angie's back. I want you to hang on while I get her ready, okay? Then she'll come get you."

"Okay." The watery voice wafted in through the window with the cold, Montana air.

He straightened and moved toward the bed. "She's doing okay. She's scared, but she's holding her own. Did you get everything?"

She nodded, her mouth drier than the Sahara. "Now what?"

He snatched up one of the harnesses and started shortening the straps, making it small enough to fit Hallie. "Did you think to get your coat while you were down there?"

She shook her head in disgust. "No. I'm not really thinking."

His gaze locked on hers. "You're doing fine. Run over to my room, I've got a light jacket in the closet there. Put that on, it'll keep you warm enough. You won't be out there long. And while you're in my closet grab one of my heavy shirts for Hallie."

She ran over to his room, found the jacket and a heavy, quilted flannel shirt, ran back, jerking the jacket on and zipping it up. "Now what?"

He tossed the now tiny harness aside, picked up the bigger one and began attaching one of the ropes to it. "Strap the crampons on your feet while I get the rope hooked to your harness."

She grabbed the crampons, sat on the floor and started strapping them to her tennis shoes.

"Make them tight. You don't want them slipping around on your feet."

She nodded, pulling the straps even tighter. "How am I going to get out there? Follow the same path Hallie did?"

He shook his head, pulling the knot on the harness tight. "There's a three-inch ledge that runs along the edge of the roof. You're going to use that."

She turned, staring at him. "Three inches? Are you out of your mind?"

"With the crampons, and as long as you follow my instructions, three inches will give you plenty of purchase."

She consciously stopped thinking. She didn't know what she was doing here. Thinking was only going to make her too afraid to function. She trusted Jason to take care of her, and from this point forward she was going to let him do it. Pulling the last strap tight on the crampons, she stood up and crawled into the harness he held out.

He snapped the harness together in front of her and then attached Hallie's harness to the front of it. "Hook Hallie into this facing you. That way she can wrap her arms and legs around you to help hold you two together. More important, you won't have her legs kicking out away from your body, tossing you off balance. Got it?"

She nodded at the instructions. "How do I get to her? Walk your little three-inch ledge like a tightrope?"

He smiled at her attempt at levity. "Nope. You're going to do a semicrawl out there. You're going to face the roof, dig your toes into the snow and ice covering the ledge and lean forward enough to keep your hands planted on the roof as you move sideways down to Hallie. That'll keep any of your weight from sticking out over the ledge and tipping you in that direction." He locked his gaze on hers. "You'll be fine. I'm not going to let anything happen to you."

She nodded, refusing to let herself believe anything else. "Okay, let's go." She snatched up the heavy shirt she'd brought for Hallie and tucked it under her harness where it wouldn't get in the way.

With his help she climbed out onto the narrow ledge. The cold snow biting into her hands, she leaned into the roof the way Jason had instructed.

"Be sure to test each step before you actually put any weight on your feet. If the snow and ice kick off the ledge, do what you can to grab hold of the stone with the crampon. Got it?"

She nodded and tested her next step, digging her feet into the icy spot.

"Hurry up, Angie, it's scary and cold out here." Hallie's voice wafted over from the gargoyle.

"I'm coming, sweetie. Just hang in there." She didn't look at Hallie; she was afraid she'd lose her balance. Or her nerve. So she kept her eyes pinned to the snowy roof in front of her and kept moving sideways, digging her feet solidly into Jason's three-inch ledge.

Foot after careful foot, she moved across the roof until her toe nudged the gargoyle's solid stone side. Then she walked her hands over until her upper body was directly above the gargoyle's back and swung her far leg in front of her and over the gargoyle's back, as if she were mounting a horse.

The landing wasn't nearly as soft as a horse's back, but it was every bit as secure. Sitting on the wide stone haunch, with her legs wrapped around the mythical beast's sides, she felt quite safe despite her precarious perch. She reached forward and grabbed Hallie's waist. "Okay, kiddo, let go. I've got you."

Hallie released her grip on the gargoyle's neck and Angie pulled her to her chest. Now they sat on the gargoyle's back like two people riding double, both of them looking out through the gargoyle's cauliflower ears. Angie hugged the tiny body tight, relief pouring through her.

But that relief quickly gave way to anger. "What were you thinking? Crawling out on the roof like this?"

Hallie sniffed, holding tight to Angie's arms where they were wrapped around her little waist. "I was going to go back to Kent House. I thought we could be a family, but you didn't want me."

The statement blew Angie's anger away like so much dust, leaving nothing but guilt and sadness behind. "Oh, Hallie." She tightened her arms around the little girl, pulling her closer.

Twice, this little bundle of energy had run away because she thought Angie didn't care for her. When in fact, just like Jason, Angie would sell her soul to be able to keep her forever.

It felt so right holding her in her arms. This tiny package of precocious innocence with her Cupid's lips and her wild, curly hair. As a matter of fact, for all the strife and peril and impossibility, right now, right at this moment it seemed as though they were all exactly where they belonged in the universe. Together, here, in this house. Hallie wrapped tightly in her arms. Jason holding the lines that were keeping them safe.

How could something that felt so right be so wrong? Or was it wrong?

Did Jason know what he was talking about when he said even a week of knowing someone loved you would outweigh the pain of loss should something happen?

She'd told Jason mere minutes ago that she never should have gotten involved with him, that she'd known it would have a bad end. But would she trade the pain slicing through her now for never having known Jason at all? Jason, or Hallie?

Would her life have been better if she'd never shared a bottle of champagne in front of the fire with Jason or gone to his bed? Would she be happier if she had never made animal pancakes or played with Hallie in the attic?

Finding the answer took much less thought than she would have guessed. In fact, it took no thought at all.

She wouldn't trade those moments for anything in the world.

Hallie shivered in her arms and she pulled Jason's shirt from her harness. Helping Hallie into it, she pulled the front double over Hallie's small chest and folded the too-long sleeves over her hands to keep them warm. Then she snuggled Hallie closer, protecting her from the cold.

In the past when she'd thought of adoption she'd always thought of it in the context of being a single parent. But if she stayed here, they would be a family. She and Jason and Hallie. If something did happen to her, Hallie wouldn't be alone. She would have Jason. And as Jason had pointed out—as Angie's doctor had pointed out more than once—she might well live to be a hundred.

"What are you two doing out there?" Jason's voice snapped her out of her thoughts. "Angie, get her in that harness and get in here."

He was right. They should go in. But big questions, important questions, pounded in her brain. And somehow, this seemed the perfect place to answer them.

She leaned her head down, talking softly into Hallie's ear. "You cold, sweetie? You want to go in, or do you want to just sit here a minute? Enjoy the view. Ride the gargoyle for a bit."

Hallie snuggled back against her. "Let's stay here a minute. I bet none of the kids at Kent House have ever